OLYOKE

Vincent Endwell

Cover art by Jenna Cha
Interior Illustrations by Echo Echo
Edited by Alex Woodroe

Content warnings are available at the end of this book. Please consult this list for any particular subject matter you may be sensitive to.

OLYOKE © 2026 by Vincent Endwell

All rights reserved. No parts of this publication may be reproduced, distributed or transmitted in any form by any means, except for brief excerpts for the purpose of review, without the prior written consent of the owner. All inquiries should be addressed to tenebrouspress@gmail.com.

Published by Tenebrous Press.
Visit our website at www.tenebrouspress.com.

First Printing, March 2026.

The characters and events portrayed in this work are fictitious. Any similarity to real persons, living or dead, is coincidental and not intended by the author.

Print ISBN: 978-1-959790-53-2
eBook ISBN: 978-1-959790-54-9

Cover art by Jenna Cha.

Interior illustrations by Echo Echo.

Edited by Alex Woodroe.

Formatting by Lori Michelle Booth.

All creators in this publication have signed an AI-free agreement. To the best of our knowledge, this publication is free from machine-generated content.

Selected Works from Tenebrous Press:

Kayak—Kristal Stittle

Dear Stupid Penpal—Rascal Hartley

Clairviolence: Tales of Tarot and Torment—Mo Moshaty

Reef Life—Hazel Zorn

Puppet's Banquet—Valkyrie Loughcrewe

Casual—Koji A. Dae

All Your Friends are Here—M.Shaw

TRVE CVLT—Michael Bettendorf

A Spectre is Haunting Greentree—Carson Winter

From the Belly—Emmett Nahil

Mouth—Joshua Hull

Lumberjack—Anthony Engebretson

Posthaste Manor—Jolie Toomajan & Carson Winter

The Black Lord—Colin Hinckley

Many more titles at www.TenebrousPress.com

To Zabé—for making me want to become a better version of myself

Recovered Document No. 14: "The Missive of the Apostle Raven-Thinkers at the Gold Dawn, at the Commencement of the Ultimate Age"

Recovered from the writings of Hieronymus Johnson in Olyoke, TN. After the outbuilding fire, most of his texts were unsalvageable, and the nature of the structure was unable to be determined from those remaining. Johnson himself did not survive to explain what he had meant when he told Rosalind Frangetti that he had "borne witness to the in-foldings, the mosaic" and had returned as a "conscripted prophet."

After he was pulled from the blaze, Johnson spent three days being treated for severe burns at Baptist Hospital before finally succumbing to sepsis, thus forever committing the purpose of his portcullis to obscurity.

IT WAS THE advent of First Winter when the raven-thinkers arrived unto the ville and commenced their proclamation. See, this was in the days of Karnivale and Oats, in Celsior, when the sea was still filthy red with the blood of languids and the law of the Potentate was exercised through the land, and so the raven-thinkers then were nothing more than nuisance and vermin. They did not yet hold the esteemed position of our latter day. When they arrived, they were of indeterminate number, dressed all in black rags and vulgar glasses perched on their long probosces, and walked like a vituperation or a conglomerate to the center of the ville. There they sat, querulous, croaking their news to all the villeagers.

Vincent Endwell

The Pestulance was coming, and it was coming swift as Eurus from the East.

Now, it is the way of people that the first day of their arrival, there was quite a tumult among the ville, as questions of action and preparation were proposed and left to sit, idle and festering, on the butcherblock of the agora. Some felt it would be necessary to take their herds of nivnevnors and hurry up the river to avoid the swinging of that great staff.

Others, such as the men-at-arms of the Potentate's Emissary, considered themselves made of tougher hide than a thing of myth and legend like the Pestulance. Likewise to the infidels, Old Man Bartholomew rocked and rocked on his chair and decried those raven-thinkers. Long should be the day before we heed their claims with acclaim!, he informed those younger twinefolk and gatherering-sams who would sit on the altar-veranda and listen. Long should be the day indeed before we listen to those superannuated and abrading philosophizers in all their thistledown rags!

But there were others who could not deny that the red-frogs were indeed turning.

Before long, there came a cavalcade of sojourners from the west, striped trumpets announcing the arrival and subsequent departure of many petty kings, princes, and abbesses, borne upon palanquins of silk or dragged by wormaurochs, their three horns blowing pettily their effusence over the ville. Tumblers and acrobats came whirling on their many legs like seedpods in a gale, pausing in the ville only for brief hours before continuing their dispersal.

Horrible!, they said to those wolving-farmers who stopped to see the tumblers' eternal performance. Horrible it is to see. It has so many teeth, and eyes all bright and yellow and loose as marbles, its snout long and protruden. Its laugh! Like a choir of drowning trumpets in a gelatinous mire!

Did you see it? Inquired those villeagers.

Oh, no, said the tumblers, packing up their stilts and hoops. But we heard about it.

Those like Old Man Bartholomew assuredly regarded this concession as a forfeiture of truth. Now see, he said to those who would listen. I have never seen the Pestulance, I have never heard the Pestulance, I have lived five hundred years to the day and I can certainly say in that time, I have learned to tell reality from disreality!

Though, others in the ville muttered, it was also true that Old Man Bartholomew was a subscriber to the Remedy, which was even in that day and age well-known to do nothing but exacerbate the symptoms.

While many in the ville still deliberated and debated, a group of youth, black-cloaked like the raven-thinkers but not so disheveled, began preparations to welcome the Pestulance. For in times such as these, it is often the youth and the dissenters who must be entrusted with true action and righteousness, for those who are sunken in their convention and minuteness will never be shaken from it. Like a cockle cannot be shaken from a shell, they must be dashed upon the rocks to experience release. This was what the group, known as the Pavers, believed to be true.

In the night, they raised the banners and illuminated the windows, and waited restlessly in the shadows for the winds to blow furious from the East, which would be the sign of their acceptance and prospectance.

And so, through the actions of the few and of the small, the ville was prepared for the coming of the Pestulance.

First, there came the hot blowing of the Eastward wind, like flames over the mountains. Then came the singing of the locusts and the sprigs, unceasing and fearful. Then came the shriveling of the grass and the browning of the dirt and the turning of the red-frogs, whereupon they opened their mouths and let their tongues protrude forth into the blossoms depicted in the ancient registers.

Then at last, the Pestulance arrived, and there was moaning and wailing and cheering from those heralds who prepared its path.

Like the blind men and the elephant, the villeagers were disable to agree on what it was they saw in that great urge. Some said they saw a man astride a skeletal horse, flames in the palms of its hands. Others witnessed a fathomless mouth as a gaping entrance to the earth, lips speaking with the shudders of an earthquake. Yet others believed it was the skull of a white-deer, mouth full of more teeth than could be counted, with antlers of branches and light rising as tall as the tallest langurewoods. It came with retainers, all of whom had stone eyes.

Vincent Endwell

Many fell to their knees before it, and were swallowed by the earth. Others remained safe on the steps of the veranda-altar, and merely felt their hair shrivel and fall from their scalps and their eyelids. Those raven-thinkers who had foretold its coming happily laid themselves before it and were eaten by the ravenous mouth—all save one youth, who scrambled off to act as herald and recounter of this time of great Humanity.

Even in the red skies of its glory, there were still some who denied the Sovereignty of Pestulance. The Potentate's Emissary was threatened and terrified by this magnificent presence, and so instructed their men-at-arms to gently shoo the Pestulance from the ville. Some success was made initially, as the Pestulance responded to the phalanx by taking several steps backwards, but soon the men-at-arms found that their arms grew fatigued and the red-frogs looked more and more beautiful and soft beneath them. When they collapsed into piles of striped sleeves and spears, the Pestulance whispered softly into their mouths.

What it said is unknown to this day. What it said after, however, was known to all.

It wished to be fed.

And so, those among the Pavers acted without consultation to bring it the wolving and grape stores of the ville. This led to confrontation, as those among Old Man Bartholomew's camp thought no gift was necessary. This argument took place by the sandstone granaries, out by the arbor, as the head of the Pestulance caused skin to bake and rivulets of sweat to slide down faces and backs. Neither side was willing to budge.

This was when the first life was taken by human hands, as the lowest of the Pavers, Samson Willing stabbed Haversham the Fourth Son of Old Man Bartholomew. The bloodbath ensuing lasted for only minutes, but once it was complete, the Pestulance was more than happy to take its share. It lay sated that night in the center of the ville, venting blistering air and singing quietly within its Lung of Lungs.

When the dawn broke like pottery, however, the Pestulance demanded yet another meal. Seeing no option, it was permitted into the granary. It did not, however, enter, but locusts ate all of the stores before departing back into its lungs. It was quite cheerful as these locusts ate, speaking affably with all in the ville who could see it. It shook hands and complimented infants in their parents' arms.

After this, It declared with some humor, wagging one finger like a tree in a gale, I will still be hungry!

The Pestulance befriended those people it could find, taking dinner at their houses but not eating a thing, merely breaking their chairs and walls with its weight. The remaining people of the ville gathered that night in the tavern, enumerating their options. Some considered radical violence. Others considered flight. Still others considered that maybe it wasn't the problem that they thought it was, and it would all work itself out. Several further believed it was all a metaphor for disenfranchisement.

By morning, no course of action had been reached, and the Pestulance arrived at the door of the tavern with a smile a thousand miles long and wide as the Brimming Sea.

It is time, it declared with infectious happiness. And it began to remove the sinews from their legs and arms and the ligaments from their torsos. While some still cried woe and alack, most within their heart of hearts privately admitted that they kind of liked it. Even Old Man Bartholomew, as obstreperous as he was, found that the returning of his flesh to fire and to blood in the ultimate annihilation of all things—well, it had a certain palpable charm.

When the meal was through, the Pestulance licked its many, many fingers and picked the meat from out of its teeth, and said to its horse: I don't know, I could eat.

So have the raven-thinkers recorded, so have they all said. So may it be stated, so may it be. When it comes again, so may we all too be delivered from the fire and the yellow sky, and be returned to sinew and lining. Amen.

The Modeling Resin

It was quiet when Beth-Anne shut the car off.

She had blasted music on the drive, a new pop playlist a friend had made for her. It was aggressively upbeat, like a salesperson on commission desperate for you to fall in love with their product. It was fine. Beth-Anne never knew what to say when people asked her what artists, or genres, or even melodies she liked. Sometimes a song would hit her and it would get stuck in her head like the empty can in the backseat that she just didn't fish out.

But she needed the noise.

She took out the keys, checked her planner for the address. She really didn't need to. She'd been surprised to see the old bar on her list of cases, since she knew the owner couldn't be past sixty. But there was the elderly man who lived above the Grisham Inn, and when she'd read the notes it all came back with a strange clarity, like yellowed text sharpening through a hand-lens.

Before she went in, Beth-Anne scrubbed her face and checked her eyes in the visor mirror. She felt a perverse pride that she was getting so good at hiding the redness.

There was no one in the bar when she entered. Just a few tables were still standing, while most had been pushed to the wall. From the dust on their tops, it didn't seem like there was ever much need for them. The bar was varnished to near-black, a masterpiece of age. Behind it, the altar of Chattanooga whiskey and Kentucky bourbon was cobwebbed in place. Beth-Anne had a brief image of it as a religious thing, a priest abandoning his sanctuary for the safety of the rectory.

She wiped the sweat off her forehead, wishing the strange feeling would go away. Weird thoughts wormed their way into her brain so often lately. She hated that it was so quiet.

Vincent Endwell

"Ruby?" Beth-Anne called. Her voice fell dead as a fly in the stuffy bar. "Ms. Frangetti?" The quiet went on long enough that her heart started to flutter against the glass. Then she heard a rustling in the back, and after a moment the gray-haired white woman came out, wearing a sauce-stained apron and a blistering blue stare.

Ruby Frangetti had the voice of an old smoker and the jowls of Winston Churchill. The way she spoke, Beth-Anne couldn't be sure if Ruby was amused or furious. It was the presence that some old women had where you knew they had been through some shit, and you were maybe in awe of them, maybe in admiration, but you didn't want to draw the laser beam of their ire. Not at all.

Beth-Anne felt like an ice skater in conversation, but one on soft and chipped ice. Fast, but stumbling. "It's really good to see you again, I hope you've been well. You were the one who called about Mr. Tover, right?" She didn't know who else would have.

Ruby gave her a long look, and a single nod in reply. She sat Beth-Anne down at the table and turned down the radio until it was just a low murmur of voices by the lace-lined window. Beth-Anne perched, taking in the unchanging decoration of the kitchen. There was the rooster clock, just like she remembered. The lace curtains, the little 6-by-6 inch television mounted under the counter to entertain a cook, or a child.

She had spent a lot of time here as a child, more than she remembered. After school, before piano lessons, Ruby and Ruby's mother would keep an eye on the sisters at the back of the bar. None too closely, but the Morrison girls had been good kids.

Mostly. Mostly good kids.

"Haven't seen him for days," Ruby said. Her sleeves were rolled up due to the heat, and there was something simmering on the stove, a slow, glooping boil. She didn't seem concerned with it. "You know, I usually don't see him for days. He's a recluse. That's what you call it when an adult is shy." She made a sound in her throat that was anywhere from a scoff to a cough.

Beth-Anne laughed noncommittally. Social work was a lot of playing both sides. Making people feel attended to, respected, understood, and yes, sometimes funny. A delicate line. "Well, how long would you say it's been since you saw him?"

Ruby shrugged like a car hood opening. "A week. Maybe two."

"Two weeks?" Beth-Anne tried to keep incredulity out of her voice. "You usually see him more than that." No confirmation. "You're acting as his caretaker at the moment, is that true?" All judgment was carefully scraped from her voice. The man had to be pushing eighty; Beth-Anne would have to talk through a solution if it turned out he wasn't capable of living on his own. That was always a discussion people loved to have.

"I bring him dinner, yeah," Ruby said. "Doesn't want much to do with me otherwise."

"Is it possible he could have gone out without you noticing?"

Another shrug. Beth-Anne tried to keep steady. She'd always been nervous of Ruby. A big, brusque lady, she was quicker with criticism than most people were with a hello. While Mrs. Frangetti always could pull on sweetness, Ruby never seemed happy to have kids underfoot. Beth-Anne remembered one moment acutely, in which Beth-Anne had showed her a school art project, a macaroni sun, and Ruby's perfunctory response: "That's all you did?"

That had stuck with her for years, although it was stupid and small and Beth-Anne knew it. It was probably why she had never shown anyone except her sister her models. She liked her paintwork, and she liked how a diorama came together bit by deliberate bit—but she never once mistook them for *good*.

"Well, my room is right by the base of the stairs, so I would have noticed. But you can think whatever you want," said Ruby. Definitely defensive. Or maybe on edge.

"Okay," said Beth-Anne lightly, and made a few notes. Ruby's room was the one that had once belonged to Mrs. Frangetti before she passed. "Just checking, that's all. And you said you've knocked on his door, but haven't gone inside. Is there a reason you haven't gone in?"

Ruby glanced away and gave another of those scoff-coughs. It was a hard look to read. One wouldn't think such a woman could be sheepish. "Don't know. Didn't feel right, Bethie."

Beth-Anne had been starting to think Ruby hadn't remembered her. A strange feeling passed over her, like a cobweb on the back of her neck.

The hallway was familiar, but in the way half-remembered dreams are. One knows that they've been there before, but the width is off, the length is shorter than it should be. The colors are at once a darker shade of wood, but don't absorb the light as deeply.

Beth-Anne was struck by how they must have looked. Two little girls, bored with their homework, peering more and more often down that long, shadowy hall. She'd always worn her hair in pigtails, with blue-framed glasses that made her look like a frog. Beth-Anne had envied her sister for her style and confidence—though the early-aughts pooka shell necklace would do no one favors anymore, now, would it.

But it had been Beth-Anne who dared her to go down into the hallway. To just explore a little. Just as far as the first door. Just don't step on any of the creaking boards. Just be quick.

They'd only gone a little the first day. Just a few steps in.

The hall was musty, the scent of old wood and dust that's worked itself into the fibers of the thin brown carpet. Ruby led the way, stopping briefly in her room for the keys. Beth-Anne remembered pausing at the base of those long steps up, distant and uncharted territory to a child's eyes. It had all been so exciting. So transgressive. Explorers in an unknown land, with secrets behind every door.

No one had ever told them they weren't *allowed* to explore.

"Do you remember when me and . . . " Beth-Anne felt her throat catch, and quickly pivoted. A neat cross-over. Ruby found the keys amidst doilies and knitted dolls in a sideboard. "Do you remember when we would hang out here as kids?"

Ruby let out a short breath. This one was amused; Beth-Anne was getting the hang of this woman. "Of course," said Ruby. "Every Thursday. You and Carly always wanted Mom's sloppy joes."

Beth-Anne leapt skillfully over that name, dodging its meaning entirely.

"Hah, I forgot about that," Beth-Anne said. "She was always cooking sloppy joes. And she would always give me lettuce on it, even though I never ate it. It was nice of her to take care of us. I know Mom always appreciated it."

A long pause. Ruby fished out the keys and double-checked the label on them. There were many keys in that drawer. "Mom liked kids," Ruby said, flat as scraped concrete. "Don't know why. She hated me."

The skate caught in a pockmark in the ice and there was a

stumble and pinwheeling of arms. Beth-Anne tucked her lips into her mouth. Better to say nothing, and let them both gracefully recover.

It had taken the sisters a month of exploring to climb the mountain. They were both scared, was the thing. They had mapped out the lower floors in the back of a school notebook, but they hadn't gone up the stairs until there was truly nowhere else to sneak around. They'd even peeked their heads into Mrs. Frangetti's bedroom, though only for a moment, just enough to pencil a rectangle onto their map.

The hesitation was because they knew about the tenant.

He *was* a recluse, as Ruby had said, though their mother had called him a shut-in. It wasn't fair, perhaps, because he had only been Mrs. Frangetti's age when they were kids, sixty or so. Nevertheless, Beth-Anne had been so scared of him. Not because of what he might be, or do, but because to see him meant that they were *really* going to get into trouble. She'd convinced herself that exploring was okay, if they were careful, and only did a little at a time.

But they'd run out of places to explore.

She remembered persuading her sister, bit by bit. Beth-Anne was usually the rules-follower, to a fault, but this was the one thing she felt she *needed* to go against. They'd spent time huddled at the kitchen table, convincing themselves that they needed to go and look. Just a few steps, they agreed. Just a few steps.

The thing was, as a kid, Beth-Anne had wanted there to be a secret. She had wanted there to be something mysterious up there. She was always looking for a mystery, like in her Nancy Drew books, or the Boxcar Kids. There was always *something* up the mysterious stairs, and Beth-Anne wanted it.

No, she *needed* it. Because that would be the world's little promise to her that things would be okay. It would *mean* something.

Beth-Anne didn't really want to know about mysteries anymore.

Ruby made her way up the stairs very slowly. A knee seemed to be giving her trouble, and the smoker's lungs certainly weren't helping. Beth-Anne followed at a respectful distance, remembering how the hall had hovered like a dark cloud above them. Each step had smelled less like the smoke of the bar, and more like a spice they couldn't place, and an earthiness she'd never smelled anywhere else.

That smell was still here. Her heart beat faster, like a metronome with the weight pulled down. Tick-tick-tick-tick-tick.

A freak illness, precipitated by environmental toxins.

That hadn't been exactly what the doctors said, it had been something more technical, but the *freak* part had been said by someone, and it had stuck in Beth-Anne's mind. That was the phrase she turned over and over while she was recovering, her parents in and out with light soups and funny stories about the wildlife outside the Food Lion. Beth-Anne had inherited their ability to never admit that anything was wrong, when one daughter was in the hospital and one was weak and feverish with a throat raw from vomiting.

It had been something to do with the models. Carly and she had started making them after their grandfather had died and they had reconnected with one other. It had been Carly's idea to buy the first model kit, just something to do while drinking wine, but they both came to really like it. Something about applying meticulous spots of paint to bring a figurine to life, and sealing it all with a topcoat to keep that paint clean and sharp forever just really did it for her.

Soon they were making whole scenes, mostly movie replicas or video game settings. A lot of superheroes, because they both liked those movies. Their last finished project was a saturated fantasy city, with tiny people in the streets and buildings painted all crimson and silver. Beth-Anne thought she enjoyed it because it gave her a sense of control—a little world all in her hands, where everything could be still and small and easily manipulated. The more she thought about it, though, she wondered if she didn't like it because of how it was *sealed*. Each scene was a singular moment literally glued in time, and each figurine itself was coated in that clear topcoat like a protective skin.

It wasn't just that things were kept in, but that things were kept out: age, dust, and decay were otherworldly forces that couldn't quite press through. They were driven back by this simple thing— a coat of clear, sealing resin.

It wasn't the paint, she didn't think. It might have been the ventilation, or it might have been the basement. But Beth-Anne was so sure it was the resin.

They'd been working together in the basement for hours the night before they got sick. And they got sick at the same time, and in such a similar way to how they had when they were young. And her sister had gotten so much sicker than she had, so much faster. Beth-Anne thought she'd gotten the flu while her sister was being rushed to the ER.

And maybe it was a fever-dream, but she would have sworn that she smelled that heady, incense-smell in the basement that night.

Carly had ordered the new resin from the internet, and they'd been excited to try it. It was from a region and tree they didn't recognize, somewhere called Blessed Well. It had seemed so exotic in its amber-brown bottle, though it said it was shipping from somewhere else in Tennessee.

They had been going to make something different with it, wooden figurines that were far more serious a craft than their usual media characters. They had been talking about making a diorama of a historical moment for the town's Hundred Bells celebration.

It would be the shape and construction of a Christmas pyramid, with old-fashioned wooden dolls varnished to look like the pioneers who first found the hot-water spring. Candles would symbolize the heat of the springs, and cabins and pioneers would be arrayed on the top. The turning fan blades would emerge from the top of 'Spirition, the town's most recognizable landmark. The sisters had drawn out all the plans, the other features all laid out. They had only just started to apply resin to the dolls.

Carly had been the only one to get it on her hands.

Beth-Anne had thrown away the resin that night. She hadn't been thinking clearly, hadn't considered that the doctors might want to do toxicology. In the end, it didn't really matter.

The doctors didn't tell her what happened to Carly. They'd talked to her parents and Carly's husband, and they'd been so upset that doctors thought it just shouldn't be mentioned to her. At the time,

Beth-Anne hadn't minded. It was enough to know that Carly was dead. She didn't need to know the grisly details. She was already traumatized, weeping uncontrollably whenever it got too quiet.

But over Christmas, in the kitchen as it got late, her mother had let it slip. They'd had some wine, but the music was low, and the missing presence of Carly felt like a mirror that you think is another room.

It wasn't that Carly just got sick like Beth-Anne. She had putrified. Liquefied beneath the skin—and the skin, which had dried and split like a skin on pudding. Mom had had to sit down and have a glass of water, her face red as a sign saying Danger! Don't Go In Here! Stop Asking Questions!

You couldn't buy that resin online anymore. The retailer had shut down not long after.

That phrase, that image—*skin on pudding*—had carved through Beth-Anne's mind like a burning iron, like a chisel in balsa wood. Whenever it popped back up, it did another loop, deepening the horrible thought.

The worst thing was the guilt.

"Always kept to himself," Ruby said. Filling the silence. Beth-Anne appreciated it, needed it. Couldn't take the thoughts that crept in. "Let's be honest, he's always been an odd bird. Came up to Mom when I was still pretty young and said he had to rent this room. Not wanted to—*had* to. The location was right, was what he said. Still sticks in my head as being, he didn't just mean for a job. I think it might have had to do with who owned the building before Mom."

"Interesting." A versatile word. "Family?"

Ruby shook her head. "He didn't have any family we ever met. Maybe he'd cut them off, maybe they were dead. They never visited. Had some friends by in the early days, but they only ever seemed to fight. Maybe they weren't friends, come to think of it." Ruby coughed, wet but unproductive. "It always seemed like he'd been through something. Gulf War, maybe."

"Did he ever have any . . . medals? Memorabilia?"

Ruby shook her head. "No. Though, come to think of it, he did have a few things with that . . . " She waved her hand. "Logo, on it. The one that looked like a lantern, I think. He had a ring with it, and that bit of stained glass in the door."

"Maybe he was in a society of some sort?"

"Yeah, something like that."

The hall was dark as she remembered. That bit hadn't been exaggerated over the years. The carpet was thick, old shag, and Beth-Anne could imagine the civilizations of mites that lived inside it, spires and castles rising and twisting only to be crushed by impossible giants. The smell grew stronger, that sick, spicy sweetness that wove through the smell of must and dirt like a snake in dry grass.

For a moment, Ruby steadied herself on the wall, and Beth-Anne had to convince herself not to flee. Rush down the stairs, hop in the car, drive until she saw the Great Smoky Mountains. The cloying smell was like a scarf around her neck, tightened and tightened oh-so-gently by someone who grins reassuringly. Someone you trust despite how light your head is getting.

The door had been so far away, down at the end of the hall, past old pictures and a table with fake flowers. A plate of colored glass stuck in the front like an old saloon or a gentleman's club, red and bloody. She and Carly had realized halfway that it was ajar.

The ribbon of crimson light that poured through. A smell that coated your mouth and lungs.

"I'm gonna look inside," whispered Carly. When she got an idea in her head, she stuck with it. That was one reason why Beth-Anne was jealous of her. Pure confidence.

"We're gonna get in so much trouble," Beth-Anne had whispered. The almost-completed map was still clutched in her hands, the designated cartographer. She had wanted to finish it so badly, but something about that door with that design etched in the glass. Maybe it was fear of punishment. Maybe that was all it was. "Let's go back."

Carly had been annoyed. "You were the one who wanted to do this, Bethie. Don't be a scaredy-cat."

"But I *am* a scaredy-cat." She had hated how petulant she sounded.

"No, you're not. You're the bravest girl I know. You're just like Nancy Drew." Carly gave her that big-sister grin. When Carly was confident, everything was going to be fine. She had been like that about her husband, about Beth-Anne's master's program, about their present for their parents' twenty-fifth. It all worked out.

Beth-Anne missed that confidence. She was so miserable without it.

The light still shone scarlet through that pane of glass. Beth-Anne remembered the blood on her hands after wiping her mouth, and tried to remember her breathing. She was doing her job. She was an adult. She was in control, just like with the models. As if everything was small and neatly in her hands. Ruby fumbled with the keys, jingling loudly.

"I just wanted to wait until someone else was here," Ruby said. Her voice was quicker than it had been. Just a little fracture in the ice. "It just seemed best to me. Have someone here who knows what they're doing. That's just what I thought. Seemed alright."

The door popped open with the stickiness of hot varnish. The spiced smell hit her nose like a wave.

She remembered red velvet. Curtains. High-backed chairs, like a dining room. Lights on a table.

It was hot in the room. The curtains were a deep red, and only a scrap of blistered light came through, casting a dim light over the mess. Cardboard boxes, newspapers. Unwashed plates stacked near the door, waiting for Ruby's return. Ruby waited outside the door, looking at Beth-Anne expectantly. *Isn't this your job?*

"Mr. Tover?" Beth-Anne was so good at keeping her voice light and even. Dancing around those chips in the ice. She groped for a light switch but couldn't find one. "Hello?"

"It's in the next room. A nutjob wired this place," muttered Ruby. That hot dread crept up in Beth-Anne, like blood pooling in her stomach and in her chest. She was going to have to go in blind. Okay. She'd just feel her way to the curtains, open the windows. Get some light that way. Dread caught in her lungs and throat like a clot.

"Mr. Tover, it's Beth-Anne Morrison here with Ruby," she called once more. "I'm here from social services. Just here to see how you're doing. I'm just going to open these blinds, I'm sorry if I'm waking you . . . "

A wash of red as the girls had prodded open the door. Just a peek. It would just be a little look. Just to finish the map. They had to finish the map if they were to solve the Mystery of the Open Red Door. The Mystery of the Man Upstairs.

The first thing that had hit them was the smell. It was gluey, heady, like paint or varnish. Beneath it was a lemon-sharp bite, and something cloying, like milk gone sour. What struck them next was the contraption sitting on the table, turning slowly like a carousel. A tiered wooden diorama built on a turning wheel. Four little candle flames sat at its base, and above it, protruding from the top, were a spire and a fan. The fan turned slowly, turning the diorama with it in a little show. A Christmas pyramid, she later learned it was called, and she had to wonder if this was why Carly had tried to make it years later. If it had stuck in her mind the same way it did in hers.

Little models posed on the tiers of the carousel. Little wooden people, stained dark with dripping varnish, stood about in Dutch girl clothes: holding hands, doing work, dancing, and singing. Beth-Anne remembered thinking that they were frozen, preserved, trapped in their little poses.

And she remembered the man. He had been what made her gasp, because she hadn't thought he would be *right there*. He looked at them from across the table like he had expected that the two of them would be visiting. His graying hair was combed back, and his jaw square and stubbled. He had nodded at them, and pointed with a meticulous paintbrush at two of the figures on the tiered device, yellow-haired girls clasping hands as if fused together.

"Look," he said, and Beth-Anne's stomach had crawled like spider fingers. "They're just like you."

Beth-Anne's hands trembled as she felt her way through the room. She could see only the outlines of obstacles: the littered trash, a set of slippers, a pillow thrown. A broken glass. A tossed table. The smell wormed up her nose, transporting her back a thousand years.

"Mr. Tover?" Her voice caught now, just a hitch. Just a little stumble. It was so quiet. It was so quiet she could hear the hum of electricity, the *thud-thud-thud* in her ears as her blood fought to be free of its veins. With relief she reached the drapes, and seized them in both hands. She squinted, and cast them wide.

There was a moment before she heard Ruby's garbled shout. She spun, pressing back against the window.

It was standing so close to her.

She must have just brushed by it, just missed it with her groping hands. It was a man. But he was made all of gray dust and hair, bits of paper and short frayed threads. Not human things. There was a sort of sheen covering its surface, like a resin, or a skin that was so fine and preserved it was like a translucent glass.

One arm was half-raised. The head—and its varnished shining face—was turned, just barely, to look at her, as if it had turned in the darkness. The eyes were all dust behind the preserved mask.

As the sun hit it, the resin started to crack. She heard it like mice in the drywall, like the drying of paint on a model left too long beneath the drying lamp. Dust started to flutter away, quicker and quicker, until there was a cloud of it like flies stirring in the attic. There was a sloughing, like dead skin coming off.

The knees went first, then the arms, then the torso. The head fell like clay and shattered. Skin and skull and teeth crumbled until all that was left was dust. Dust, and the somber resin face of a man who had been younger when it was painted.

The Wandering Daughter

r/Hailey Land Theme Park and Destination

Posted by u/**kendrick_last** · 6 years ago
I am a former Hailey Land employee, AMA!
I worked at the Temple for 3.5 years, 1 in the Waltzing Wax Museum, the rest as a rollercoaster operator.

lmao_reddit_is_garbage · 6 years ago
Do they really have a Hailey Land jail?
    kendrick_last · 6 years ago
    Lol, yes. It's mostly for drunks to sober up

redhawksman · 6 years ago
Are there secret tunnels?
    kendrick_last · 6 years ago
    Yes! Although five are off-limits (due to safety concerns). Under the main park, all the buildings are connected so that performers and vendors can get from theaters/dressing rooms to different parts of the park without ruining the illusion for the guests.

    A buddy and I explored them while we were

VINCENT ENDWELL

looking for a place to smoke one time, and you can get all the way from the Bucking Broncos Ampitheater to the Stampede without ever seeing sunlight, although the route gets kind of roundabout because nothing goes underneath 'Spirition.

handsomebadger · 6 years ago
whats the best way to have sex in the park?
    kendrick_last · 6 years ago
    See above. I don't recommend it, though, because some poor idiot like me is going to have to see that shit. Also then you're boning in a creepy tunnel.

4lexa · 6 years ago
Is it true Hailey Land can't legally sell you alcohol?
    kendrick_last · 6 years ago
    Yes, 100%. Which is why they make sure not to call it alcohol. Go to any bar, and order the drink *not* labeled "virgin," and you're good to go.

    handsomebadger · 6 years ago
    so they can sell booze, but they can't call it booze??? why tf??
        kendrick_last · 6 years ago
        Basically, there are a bunch of old laws from the revival that never got taken off, so nowhere in Olyoke limits is technically allowed to sell anything named alcohol, but they're allowed to sell it if they name it something else. No one enforces this or anything, so places will sell you "lemonade"

OLYOKE

and "virgin lemonade," or "grape beverage" and "non-alcoholic grape beverage" instead of wine. I don't get how this isn't more of a liability than simply selling alcohol, but I can only assume that there are like 3 revivalists in city hall that this makes happy, so who knows. This is also why Olyoke is one of the only places where you'll regularly see "malt water" on the menu. Go figure.

ScarletBeth · 6 years ago
What was the weirdest costume you had to wear?
    kendrick_last · 6 years ago
    I was a Union standard bearer in the racist show at the Stampede. Better than being the other guys, but, jesus.

redhawksman · 6 years ago
How much did you make? What caused you to no longer work there?
    kendrick_last · 6 years ago
    1. Seven twenty-five an hour, baby. Love that Tennessee minimum wage.
    2. The wax museum burned down and that seemed like a good a time as any to quit.

MemphisMom · 6 years ago
What's the secret best thing to do in Hailey Land?
    kendrick_last · 6 years ago
    Get the cinnamon bread at the Grist Mill. 1) It's made off-site, which makes me actually trust it. 2) It's delicious. 3) Buy me some.

Vincent Endwell

lucyxgabriel · 6 years ago
Why do people who work there call it the Temple?
> **kendrick_last** · 6 years ago
> b/c the place makes you deeply weird if you work there long enough.
> Actually tho I think it's some word play. Hailey Land is a (bad) pun on Holy Land ("Come journey to the Hailey Land! Fun for the Whole Family"), so it's just one leap from Hailey Temple to the Temple. The original owner was also a revival preacher, so there's definitely something weird going on there.

itsmeamee · 6 years ago
I went to the wax museum when I was 8 and it scared the shit out of me, how was it working there?
> **kendrick_last** · 6 years ago
> Ha, yeah, that definitely wasn't an uncommon reaction. Mannequins never freaked me out too much, but that place absolutely tested my limits in an uncanny valley kinda way. One of my coworkers actually had a panic attack after going into the basement, but he was also vaguely unstable.
>
> For everyone else: To give you a feeling of what the wax museum was like, imagine sort of an uncomfortable mix between the basement of your grandma's church and a car showroom. The museum was one of the oldest spots on campus (one of the originals they co-opted in the eighties) and they hadn't gotten around to

renovating it before it burned. The entrance had that sort of beige linoleum and drop-ceiling like you'd get in a church hall, but done up with some posters and signage and lights so it wasn't too unexciting.

That's where I'd take your tickets, and then show you through a little door on the left into an expanded room. The exhibit hall was all arranged in a winding path so you could walk through, look at one wax model and the backdrops, I'd say a bit about Hailey Temple's costumery or a funny story from the set, and then we'd move on.

Most of the models were of Hailey Temple from various productions or music videos at different points in her life. We also had some other singers and famous back-up dancers (for example, one of the women in the red daisy dukes in the video for "Let Me Out").

It was a great place to work in the summer, too, because no matter how hot it was outside, you know what can't get hot? Wax. The A/C was always blasting to arctic temperatures in there, because when it broke the summer of 2008, not only did I nearly faint from heat stroke, but we had to move a bunch of the mannequins to storage in the basement. There used to actually be a ton of Hailey Temples down there—both because of that incident, and because the wax was actually finished with some kind of resin that didn't have a very good lifespan. After about seven(?) years or so, the resin on them started to yellow and crack unless it was reapplied, which none of us knew how to do.

So the mannequins would look really good and lifelike for a handful of years, after which they would start to look kind of sallow and jaundiced, and then their skin would peel like translucent paper, and we would move them to the basement. I never quite figured out what the deal was there—I think they used to have an artist who would maintain them, but maybe they left or they didn't get paid or something and stopped coming. We'd just stick them in the basement indefinitely, so it was a real horror show down there.

So yeah, if you'd come to the wax museum as a kid right before we swapped out some of the old mannequins, yeah, you probably would have had nightmares, haha.

sapphoslasthope · 6 years ago
What's the strangest thing you saw while working there?
    kendrick_last · 6 years ago
    The time a woman ran into the burning wax museum to save her "child."
        lucyxgabriel · 6 years ago
        holy fuck what
        sapphoslasthope · 6 years ago
        Oh my god, please elaborate.

OLYOKE

kendrick_last 6 years ago
Right, so, I'll tell you this story the way I tell people in bars, which is to say, I'll leave out the weirdest bits to start so you don't immediately think I'm nuts. (Sorry this is kind of long).

So, one week our air conditioning broke. A nightmare in Olyoke generally, but the heat caused whatever resin was on the mannequins to start flaking like it did when they got old. So as the temperature rose, many of the wax replicas all turned a sort of sickly yellow, and then their skin started to crack and flake, and whatever was attached to them—hair, for instance—would break off at the slightest touch. So we basically had to shut down for a few weeks.

It was shortly after this that this lady came in and told me that she needed to get in to find her daughter, who she said was hiding inside. It was strange, though; this was a few weeks after we'd gotten the AC fixed, and we were finally just setting up the exhibits again after the new models had arrived, and none of it was open yet.

This lady seemed distressed, though—she was wearing these lace gloves and head-covering, and she kept wringing her hands so that the lace made this scratching sound as she talked to me. She really did seem agitated, too, and kept glancing around like she was going to see her kid hiding behind the desk or in a doorway or something.

So I looked at my coworker, and he shrugged, and so I agreed to take her around to look for her kid. I asked why she thought her kid had come in here, but she just said she had run off. The woman spent a lot of time peering at the exhibits, though, and I started to wonder if there was some other reason she had wanted to get in—maybe to see the replicas without paying? It was all really weird. She spent a *lot* of time in particular looking at one mannequin of Hailey Temple in her blue sequined cowboy outfit from "Cry For Help," which was one of the ones that got melted and we replaced.

We got through all the exhibits, including the extremely long exhibit for "This Is Not A Song", and there wasn't any kid. The lady seemed to be looking around even more now, and asked if we had any other rooms. I said no, because the only other spaces were our breakroom and the basement, and both of those we kept locked.

Then she started to get angry with me, saying that there had to be another room because she was *sure* her child was here. My coworker Trevor came in to see what was going on, and I just had to insist that it really seemed unlikely that her kid was in here. I asked what her kid's name was and what she looked like so we could check again and call out, but she wouldn't tell me. She just said she wanted to check the other rooms.

Finally, Trevor suggested that we call campus security to look for the kid, and the woman put her hands to her head, let out a gut-wrenching sob, and then told us we were heartless and didn't care. Then she left.

So that was a strange experience, definitely. But it doesn't end there, because that woman started coming in every week. It wasn't always during my shift—the other people who worked there started seeing her, too, and had similar interactions, where she pretended to be looking for a missing child. Eventually the word got around about her, and campus security was supposed to be keeping an eye out, but somehow she kept getting into the Temple and all the way to the wax museum. It was some distinctly grade-A weird shit.

Fast forward to August. We're re-opened and the place looks better than ever, because while it was shut down we actually got to repaint and dust. I'm working register, lining people up for the next tour while Trevor takes one through. I'm checking passes when I start to notice this unusual smell. At first I think it's one of the visitor's perfumes, because it has this sort of sweet, lily-of-the-valley smell to it.

Then it started to smell sickly, like garbage on a really hot day, and I started to look around. Like, was it really this person standing before me? Because she looked normal and put-together, not like rotting meat.

That's when people started streaming from the showroom door. Trevor came out after them and grabbed my arm, and he told me to get them all out because the place was on fire.

I started ushering everyone out while Trevor sprinted off, presumably to get security. We didn't have fire alarms because I think some genius in management didn't want to disturb the tourists (definitely illegal), but it didn't take long before I a) convinced everyone they had to get outside immediately, and b) started to smell smoke. Legitimate, burning, sour smoke.

I was freaking out, obviously, but everyone got out okay, and security came running to move them away from the building. Now smoke was billowing out the front, and I still wasn't hearing sirens, because the worst thing for an amusement park is broadcasting that anything is wrong. While we were moving everyone farther back, I see someone break in the back of the crowd and sprint past me toward the building.

I started to shout, and then I realized it was that woman with the veil and lace gloves. She was running full-tilt *toward* the building, and got in the door before anyone could grab her. A security guy tried to go in after her, and then took a huge breath of smoke and started coughing. One of the other guys pulled him back, and that's when we could actually *see* the fire in the doorway.

It was another few minutes before the fire brigade arrived, and by then it was way too late. The place was going up, and all they could do was spray down the other buildings and make sure it didn't take down the whole park. It was a surreal experience, and I still don't know what possessed that woman to run back inside. Maybe she really thought her kid was in there. I don't know. It still freaks me out to this day, though. Obviously.

> **sapphoslasthope** · 6 years ago
> jesus christ wtf??? this can't be for real
> **paradise_loser** · 6 years ago
> no it's fucking real, it was in the Olyoke Sun, I literally cut it out and showed it to my friends at school
> **deadmetal** · 6 years ago
> Yeh, I'm also an Olyoke native and can attest. I knew a woman killed herself but didn't know all this. Totally wi . . .
> [see more replies]

redhawksman · 6 years ago
You said there were wierder details you left out, are you gonna tell us?

> **kendrick_last** · 6 years ago
> Oh, yeah. Right. Well, you asked for it.
> —So, one time after she left, I actually followed the woman to see where she went. Not far, I wasn't creepy about it, but it was already weird that she got into the Temple practically weekly when security was looking out for her, and I just wanted to see if she was hiding on campus somewhere we could find.
>
> She took a few streets through the park until she finally ended up at 'Spirition, and went

inside. Well, that took me aback, but I followed her in—there's usually a line, but that day there wasn't, and she'd gotten right in.

Then I had a choice, because while everyone always goes up in 'Spirition to look at the view, there's also a stair that leads down—not too far, it's usually locked, but that seemed like a more likely spot for her to be hiding than up with the tourists. So I went down and looked around the little room down there, and tried the door (locked), but there was no one there and no sign of anyone staying down there. And I already knew the tunnels didn't connect there.

Not even a minute later, I went up. But there was no sign of her, though there were people going up the stairs, coming down, and no one claimed to have seen her. I got all the way to the top before I was pretty sure she wasn't there.

It's possible she could have dodged me, and no one else saw a woman in a veil and gloves. People aren't that observant. But, it was still weird.

—One thing I only remembered/realized years after the place burned down was that we actually had the original mannequin in the basement. Before the Temple first opened, the artist had only done one replica that was displayed in the front hall of the theater. Hailey

Vincent Endwell

Temple apparently liked it so much that when the Temple opened, she commissioned more and made it her own exhibit.

We'd had that original in the basement for years, though, because it had the same problem where the resin peeled and became yellow and misshapen, and it wasn't good to look at. We actually kept it under a sheet way in the back.

The funny thing was, though, that replica wasn't of Hailey Templeton.

It was actually of the artist's granddaughter.

On The Fire

When I speak of the fire, some think that I am being metaphorical. This is a fair confusion, given I am a writer prone to embellishment and flourish, but let me be plain with you now: when I speak of the fire, I am speaking in nothing but the most literal terms.

The fire is coming. It is not coming soon, but it is coming *swiftly* upon all of us. It does not move with any speed—is always the same distance away in every moment, but that distance grows closer and closer with each turn of the celestial meter. As Hieronymus explains, we are subject to more than one time, yet we are relentlessly pulled by them forward into many futures. These gusts of time are like buffeting winds, or different forces acting upon the Christmas pyramid of our world.

When I speak of the Christmas pyramid, some think I am being literal. In this instance, I speak in metaphor, a metaphor created by King Hieronymus to explain to his counselors what he saw in the land beyond dreams, where he was conscripted like a prisoner into prophecy. Imagine the joyful Christmas pyramid, which stands on a tiered carousel, decorated with dioramas of city and field, country and street. We are like little wooden dolls on the lowest layer, obliviously turning about and about in our lives. They do not know that their world is circular and flat, nor do they recognize that it spins and ferries them about. We experience time the way the dolls experience the revolutions of the level, both imperceptible yet inexorable. It drags us around and around the same heavenly revolutions in that deterministic machinery of the planets.

There is another force, however, that acts upon the Christmas pyramid. That is the flame of the candles at its base. The dolls do not understand the candles, nor do they understand how it is the pyramid turns, but it does. The heat from the candles rises and turns that great wooden fan at the top, and so spins our world through the fourth axis of time. This is like a force from another world to the dolls, who cannot see the flames, only feel the turn and feel the heat, melting the wax and glue of their little bodies, warping the world through the haze of smoke.

It is this that Hieronymus knows is coming—the rising heat, which warps and shifts and transfigures. Like the dolls, we have no escape from the flames that will consume us—unless we escape to a higher level. In his prophecy from the lands beyond, Hieronymus sees the second level. It is this level that we must aspire to rise to through whatever means. It is only through ascension, and integration into this new and higher realm, that we can possibly evade our fate at the hands of the fire.

And here I must decry the falsehoods of the Colonel, who has led far too many astray on his liar's path. He fails, either through stupidity or malice, to understand the layered construction of the worlds. Neither does he care from which direction the fire comes—below or above or all around us, none of this matters to him. He believes that the fire will be a scouring force, a cleansing event, and that which has been adequately preserved will be purified and released into a burnished, perfect earth. This delusion is beyond foolishness and must be recognized as an active tool of manipulation and danger to all around him. Already he has swayed far too many to his path—including some of our number—and they go about "preserving" that which cannot be saved, at great cost. While I have my dark suspicions as to why he has promoted this incorrect belief, suffice it to say he is a fool and a traitor, and all should be warned against listening to his honeyed words.

To all who have come to understand Hieronymus' scientific message, I say, remember what he wrote upon visiting the world beyond dream for the third and final time, before he began his construction. He wrote that in his journeys beyond, he witnessed many worlds. And in one of these worlds, these potentialities stretching above and below us and out every direction like the spokes of a grand wheel, he saw the worm people of the swamp, as we also have in our world. Here they lived with a race of giants before whom Hieronymus stood like a child, and when they ran the giants shook the ground and churned the water. The worm people told him, as he clung to his raft in the bog, that when the fire came the giants would bury their heads, and drink the water that would quell the fire, and their people, meaning giants and worms alike, would be transfigured by its heat from worms into frogs.

Hieronymus warns us to be not like the worm people. We cannot hide our heads beneath the water, and we cannot become warped beyond recognition by the heat which rises even now. Hieronymus implores us: we must climb to the second level. We have all of time in which we must do it, because the fire is so very close.

—E. Haskill, 1962

SCRATCH

KIDS NEVER REALIZED how easy it was to hurt grown-ups, you know?

Kids thought adults were perfect stoics, indifferent as mud; but adults were hurt just as much by harsh words and sharp glances. Sure, you got a thicker skin as time went on, obviously, but it wasn't like things couldn't cut through. You just had to keep on and swallow your salt.

It wasn't really fair, in a way.

Caroline hadn't been a teenager in years, but Darcy felt as defensive and angry as she had been during those times of barbed comments and slammed doors. After Caroline left, Darcy took off on the trail up through the woods, her walking stick chunking in the dirt as she replayed years of sneers, jibes about her out-of-style clothes, barked insults when she had offered snacks to her friends.

It had stung then, and it stung again now when Caroline was on her about the dishes, the counters, brushing the dog, whatever. You know, she got it, she really did. She was a gross old woman and no one should want to be around her. She got it. Caroline didn't have to rub it in. Magpie snuffled around in the dirt, and didn't seem to notice Darcy scrub the tears from her face. Even the dog didn't give a shit. Yeah, wasn't that just like it?

After walking a while, Darcy felt a little better, though her throat started giving her shit. She'd spent too many years on her feet when she was a waitress at Hailey Temple's Country Corral—flirting with customers and rolling her eyes with the other impersonators through clouds of cigarette fumes out by the back fence—that it didn't feel right to be sitting down, even with her smoker's lungs. At an hour out, the heat of anger had subsided, though there was still a sting like a curling iron on your skin.

OLYOKE

Caroline was just a busybody, was all. She just always had to be telling someone what to do. Darcy didn't know where she got it from, but she guessed she couldn't get enough of it with Rob, so it had to be telling her mother that the fridge wasn't clean, throw everything in it away (it was perfectly good), and don't go out except for groceries, and don't touch your face with unclean hands. The implication being, of course, that her mother was a slob. It was all just part of Caroline's need for control. Really, it was her problem.

For a moment, Darcy wished she'd been nicer to her own mom, when it mattered. But then, she'd had reasons. So who knew?

When Darcy went out on walks, she brought with her a crinkling plastic bag in case she found anything interesting, and also a knife, just generally a good thing to have in the country. Sometimes she found animal skulls, or bits of trash that had weathered well, or sometimes she just got bored and went into town and did the shopping. Today, she was well away from town, and so she was surprised when she came across a brick building in the woods. Smeared with moss and windows boarded up, it grinned like an eyeless mouth through the trees.

Though the path to the front was packed dirt, around the back of the building—an old schoolhouse from the revival days, maybe?—a pond was eating at the foundation. Sinking, muddy, and shot with yellow reeds, the water washed right up to the base, leaving only the narrowest walkable strip between the two. Darcy took it carefully, and bits of mud slipped and slid back into the water like peeling skin.

Magpie sniffed and rolled into the water, her matted fur giving her the look of an armored boat. She'd always been a swimming dog. She milled about for a while as Darcy watched. Yellow seaweed swayed beneath the surface of the pond, rolling with the ripples.

Wait, that wasn't right. Darcy crouched stiffly, her back giving her shit now too. Reaching out with her stick, she prodded the seaweed, and paused. It wasn't seaweed at all. It was a bunch of long, fat worms.

Yellow-white and about the size of her wrist, they squirmed as if they could see her hand as she waved it back and forth through where they drifted. Dark eyespots on their heads stared like single eyeballs where they grew up like tubers from the pond muck.

This wasn't something Darcy had ever seen before. She watched them for a while as Magpie splashed around along the shore; all the while the urge to pull one out grew stronger and stronger. She was a little surprised that she was able to reach in, grab one, and yank until it popped out like a hair from a follicle. Out of the water, it coiled and writhed around her hand, first vigorously, then slowing to a languid curl. It felt oddly like warm pasta, and its color shifted from raw dough at the head to yellow-onion at the base. Little trailing cilia came from the end that had been in the muck, like the roots of a bulb.

Darcy wasn't sure why she decided to harvest them. Maybe it was that she didn't earn much in tips anymore. Maybe it was that Hailey Temple was well past the days of her popularity, and maybe it wasn't like Paul's pension had ever been anything to sniff at anyway, so why did she even bother with it except that it came in the mail and she didn't have to think about it?

Maybe it was that the worms were fat and heavy like uncooked bread, and Darcy couldn't help but think they wouldn't be bad if she cooked them right.

Rolling up the legs of her jeans as far as they could go, Darcy waded into the water and dug up a set. They sunk into the plastic bag nicely, and by the time she got enough, the ones at the bottom had nearly stopped squiggling around.

Magpie's snout dripped just above the water, her eyes brown and free of judgment.

By the time she reached the house, all the worms were dead. They stuck together, limp and soggy as she washed them off, their gray eyespots staring up at her like the worms were dead fish at the market. She fried them in the pan with butter, breadcrumbs, and a doctor's dose of onion powder, and then piled them on a plate like fat pasta. They smelled interesting, hearty and cloying, and she carved off a piece and hesitated with it before her lips.

It smelled like flour; butter and onion overpowered it, but beneath it there was that floury smell, and something like overcooked egg whites. There were little grainy bits in them, too, she discovered as she pushed them around with a fork. Bits of gray clustered inside and scraped like sand against the plate. And there was something else.

They had little mouths. She had missed that before. There were thin lines on their pointed heads—not quite a jaw, exactly, but a curved opening like they were all smiling up at her. Shame grew in her gut: what would her daughter say? Was she supposed to eat these; did these little smiling worms know what fate was coming? Not to mention Caroline's look of disgust would be like a punch to the gut. As if Darcy hadn't raised her on frog's legs and venison jerky, but Caroline had always been so particular. Always so much *better than.* Ever since she was a kid.

Darcy's fork hovered above the plate, her hand trembling ever so slightly. Then with a sharp movement, she put the plate down on the floor and put her head in her hands. Magpie came over and gleefully scarfed down the meal, red tongue licking the muzzle that protruded from within her helmet of hair.

When Darcy went to get her chipped nails redone, it was weird how seriously some people were taking the reem. It came around once when she was a kid, but maybe she just didn't remember how scared people had been. Now, people were in homemade veils and gloves, and others gave them vicious glances as they passed by. Even some restaurants were closed, signs in the windows reading, "Takeout only," or "Until further notice," or "Infected! Do not enter!"

In the salon, even Kelsey was wearing blue rubber gloves and a veil, her blue eyes red and watery through the mesh.

"You didn't get it, did you?" Darcy asked, and Kelsey shook her head.

"Allergies," she said. "I get them bad in the springtime."

"Well, hallelujah," Darcy said. "I'd be so P.O.'ed if you were closed, I'd have to drive to Chattanooga."

"We thought about it," Kelsey said flatly. "But we'd go out of business, so." She shrugged, polish hanging off the tip of her brush like a clotted drop of blood.

Vincent Endwell

Darcy's vision felt blurry on the drive home, enough that she had to stop and scratch her eyes—delicately, with the newly done nails. She had put off getting glasses for nearly five years, but maybe it was finally time. It felt like another admission of getting old and irrelevant, and it was stupid, but it crossed her mind whether Leo (who was working now at the All-In-One) would still want to see her if she had glasses, and whether Caroline was going to tease her for them as well.

The worst part was that even after all these years, her mother's voice leaked out. The one that said she should wear polish and then called the color tacky. The one that sounded like the click of managerial heels, the pop of a lipstick tube. It sounded like holding still just so until she was prodded into shape.

She'd done the pageant circuit when she was younger, just like Mom had, and she knew the space she was supposed to stay in so well—the zipper-cinched space between "ugly" and "fake." Once she'd walked it like a swaying tightrope, and for years the rope had been getting slacker, and the fall more and more final.

A few tears leaked out, just a couple, but years of waitressing had taught her to be sure the makeup stayed on at all costs. Her eyes were only a little red when she checked the mirror, and the blue of her eyeshadow was still sharp as a pin.

In the years since, she'd swung toward ugly, and she'd swung toward fake, and it had felt freeing as hell, honestly, to finally be done with that old bitch and all her little barbs. But maybe the bitch wasn't wrong, though, because every time, the fall still hurt. Even when she braced for it.

Maybe this was it, though. Maybe she was "clinging to the past," like they said. Like those older women who still dressed like they were in their twenties, who she had always sneered at. "Who does she think she's fooling?" she had said of her mom at forty, still in a tight skirt and an updo coiled like a reed basket on her head. Pushing fifty-sixty now, though, she felt it.

She felt it, because what else was there? Everyone seemed to be saying, "age gracefully." But there was no graceful aging when all that meant was, "be ugly, so we can ignore you. Be as ugly and gross as we think you are, so we never have to deal with you again."

When Caroline came by again, she sighed at the pan on the floor and the dishes in the sink, and got started on cleaning them up. Her lecture about sanitation—"the reem's going around, you actually have to clean surfaces and your hands, not to mention you're going to get mice"—Darcy ignored, not able to deal with it. Darcy crouched by Magpie, who had been lying on her side for hours, making sort of a *whuffing* sound for the past half.

She seemed okay, just a little short of breath like Darcy always was. Darcy scratched at her eye as she waited, and patted Magpie's side. Her fur was getting pretty matted, so maybe it was the weight of all that knotted hair that was causing the problem. Of course, if she shaved it off, it would just get matted again in mere weeks. Paul had always said that dog was more trouble than she was worth, but Darcy liked Magpie—and disagreeing—so she'd argued with him. But he had been right. Magpie, like beauty, was maintenance.

"Mama, are you gonna listen to *anything* I'm saying," Caroline demanded, leaning in the doorway to the kitchen. Her hands were soapy to the wrists, and the pocket of her sweatshirt bulged with a twelve-ounce of hand sanitizer. "I told you already, *don't touch your eyes!*"

Darcy looked up with a burst of shame and anger. She wasn't going to cry in front of her daughter. She *wasn't going to*. She bit off her words between her teeth, trying to keep calm but quickly losing grip.

"I've had it up to *here* with your attitude," she exclaimed, and then it all came tumbling out. "I don't know what it is with your, your, control freak complex, but it stops. It stops right here! Do you know I spent ten hours in labor with you, ten god-damned hours! and you don't goddamn talk to me this way! You don't have a goddamn right!"

She didn't cry when Caroline left. She just sat on the brown carpet by the door, wishing she didn't feel so shitty but not regretting a single fucking thing.

Vincent Endwell

It was burning hot at night.

Darcy woke like bubbles rising through stagnant water. She couldn't remember when she had shucked off her blankets like psoriatic skin, but now she lay still, breathing, the heat pressing down like an iron lung on her chest. Shapes burned black outlines in her eyes.

"It's not your fault, you know," said a voice in the dark.

Darcy froze. It was the sort of thing where you knew no one should have been here, no one should have been in your house, but it was so sudden and awful and wrong that for a moment you just denied it. It had to be a dream. It couldn't be happening. But she *heard* it, and she knew she did, and finally that thought penetrated like a needle in a vein.

She rolled over. Her arms felt heavy as sodden sacks of meal; useless weights. The nightlight down the hall spilled through the doorway. A four-legged shape stood there, the squareness and size of a cut stone. It wheezed: in, out, in.

"You shouldn't regret the things you've done," said Magpie. Her voice was familiar as an old recording, like a Hailey Temple song she'd heard five times a shift for thirty years. "You did the best you could, you know. Sometimes life just fucks you."

Darcy wedged herself up on an elbow, her breath catching. The room was burning hot like there was a fire under it, crackling flames through the floorboards that she just couldn't see yet.

"What?" she asked, softly, not even sure she should speak. Whether talking back would just make her mad.

"I said, sometimes life just fucks you," said Magpie, and laughed a wheezing, feverish laugh. "Never mind. I'm just trying to be helpful. Maybe you don't need it, since you didn't have any problem never visiting, never calling, letting her get bedsore and septic. Good thing your bitch daughter doesn't know about that. She might get *ideas*."

"I didn't—" Darcy gasped, and then levered herself out of bed. She threw herself with heavy footfalls at the dog, and Magpie danced out of the way, circling to the other side of the bed. Her red tongue lolled and panted, and her eyes glinted wide and yellowed.

"Who told you that?"

"You're not going to ask how I can talk?" said Magpie. "Honeybun, that's a stupid question, why would you think you'd get an answer to that?"

"I don't give a shit how you can talk," Darcy wheezed. Her head felt light and her skin was hot as tarmac in the sun, hot as a can in the fireplace. "I care how—I care how—"

Magpie gasp-laughed again, a sound like brown water sputtering from a faucet. It sounded just like her old smoker's cough, just like the sound of hair yanked through a brush. "Don't worry about it, honeybun, I'm just kidding with you. I didn't mean it like that. I'm just saying, you're making it easy for her. Oh, don't you cry those tears, you big baby. I didn't mean it like that."

Something broke in Darcy, then.

"Get over here, you *bitch!*" Darcy shouted and lunged. The dog danced away, but she was too slow. Darcy's nails sunk into the matted fur and held on tight. "I'm done with you! You hear me? I never said it to your face, but *I don't goddamn need you anymore!*"

She dragged the dog down, down, through the kitchen and to the door out back. The night was far too hot, far too hot for a cold week, hot like burning jets flooded the ground beneath. Hot like a fever in your lungs.

Darcy grabbed the pan by the kitchen door and paused as she lifted it high. Magpie's eyes were yellow like onions, and the pupils were just a flat gray spot. They bulged from the sockets, extruding like fingers in latex, like ointment from a tube. They lolled down the dog's cheeks, staring and judging.

"I didn't mean it like that, baby girl," smiled Magpie.

Caroline surveyed the kitchen, an impressed look stuck on her face like paper to plaster. "Wow, Mama, nice work," she said. The counters had all been wiped, and the dishes and pan had been scrubbed and were drying in the drainer. Darcy had even taken a sponge to the stove and the microwave, she was feeling so inspired.

"Don't act so surprised," Darcy said. Her red nails had gotten chipped again, so you could see just a little bit of blood underneath.

She picked it out before Caroline could notice, and then scratched at her eye again, where the skin was puffy and red beneath the concealer. "You know my back's been killing me, and I'm actually not supposed to be doing all this work with my lungs the way they are, and you know, I did it anyway. Just because I know it drives you nuts."

Caroline looked over and sighed. A thought seemed to cross her mind, and she came over and wrapped Darcy in a hug. "I know, Mama," she said. "I'm sorry I'm always on your case. I just care about you. You know the reem's going around, and it's scary, it's like nothing I've seen in my life. I'm just always worried about—everyone. You and Rob and Teresa."

"I know, honeybun," Darcy said.

"I love you."

"I love you, too."

After a long moment, Caroline let her go. She swallowed as she straightened, like her throat had gone hard. Then she sighed. "Mama, I said don't scratch at y—"

THE MURDER IN THE MARSH

The following stories should be of particular interest to long-time Olyoke residents and tourists to the location alike. In fact, anyone curious about the Splitridge region during the "dark times" prior to the town's commercial growth should find the stories interesting. All the usual Olyoke marvels—unheeded warnings, unexplained occurrences, and of course, unrecovered missing persons—are present. Reference to the "Blessed Well" should delight any acquainted with local folklore.

I hope you will enjoy reading THE MURDER IN THE MARSH. I enjoyed researching the stories and writing them. If you have any questions or would just like to write, feel free. I'd like to hear from you. Enjoy.

E. S. Hammond
Mountain Home Terrace
Olyoke, Tennessee
June, 1999

SOMETHING IN THE WATER

The town of Olyoke is bordered to the east by the Splitridge Marsh, with which locals have had a storied relationship since the town was founded. While successful settlements have always been built on the sides of the nearby titular ridges, citizens have envied the low lands and sought to construct buildings closer and closer to the edge of the wetlands.

When construction on the theme park began in 1973, many years before the first ground would be broken, the first order of business was to drain the marshy lands adjacent to the town proper to expand the available real estate. At the time, the nearest structure to the swamp was 'Spirition, erected in 1959, and all other buildings were to the north and west. This project was to be the most ambitious in the town's history, championed by the up-and-coming Orlie Trentham of the Grand Old-Tyme, and would create a series of canals to drain over 500 acres of swamp land back into the Chattanooga River.

Within months of starting construction on the canals, however, the Grand Old-Tyme ran into complications. George Wisniewski, a foreman on the site, recalls the earliest sign of the trouble: It had been a hot day, and cicadas were buzzing outside of his office, when one of the laborers showed up pounding at his door. The man was sweating profusely and panting, and it was clear he had run for quite a distance. Wisniewski gave him a drink of water and finally got the source of the disturbance out of him—a number of the men who had been laboring down in the water were seemingly out of their minds.

Wisniewski, a practical man not given to flights of fancy, was certain it had to be heat stroke. In his signature short sleeves and tie shortened to be compatible with machinery, he went down with the worker to the water, only to find several members of his digging crew missing, and several others standing around ankle deep in muck, looking down at something. However, as he approached, he realized the object of their observation. Shapes stuck up out of the muddy water—the heads of his other men, buried up to their necks in silt and gasping in the burning sun.

Wisniewski ordered them hauled up and given a day off to recover with water and shade. The men who had burrowed themselves in the mud resisted being dug up, and Wisniewski remembers thinking it was odd that they protested by shouting that the "heat was *coming*," rather than the heat was already here. The day, as he recalled, was in the mid-nineties and as ever, drenchingly humid. Unsettling as it was, Wisniewski was sure this was a freak disturbance.

Little did he know that this sort of disturbance was to become a regular occurrence, one that would severely impact the completion of the project.

Olyoke

Thefts

Shortly thereafter, the construction site experienced a number of materials thefts around the property. George Wisniewski remembers first noticing this when going over the inventory and coming up short on concrete and metal rivets. He sent men to look around the site for the misplaced supplies, but after three searchers returned with nothing, he was forced to concede the possibility that they might have been stolen. There had been no witnesses, though, nor any obvious signs of how the theft had been carried out, despite the fact that the missing amount was not insubstantial.

At this time, the men who had buried themselves in the muck had made a recovery; all except one who had quit. But at this new event, one of the three searchers resigned on the spot. When Wisniewski asked her why she was leaving, the woman remarked that two things were too much, and she was getting out before it was too late.

Wisniewski posted night watchmen around the construction site. The digging of the drainage canal continued.

A Strange Woman

Tom Halliday is now in her mid-fifties, but she was in her early twenties when she quit her construction job for the Grand Old-Tyme. She never left construction, though, and now her business is contracted by the Hailey Temple Corporation. She says the new management is better than it used to be under the Trenthams. A broad-shouldered aging white woman with a faded sleeve of tattoos, clipped hair graying like grass in an old film, Halliday doesn't seem like the kind of person to get easily spooked.

She recounted this to me from the kitchen of her small overgrown house in Mountain Home, where she lives with her wife Pat. Green vines crawled entirely over her windows and out in the yard, an old motorbike sat wrapped beneath a tarpaulin. "I don't have much use for superstition," she told me. "I just know a cue. And I was hearing it loud and clear."

As it turned out, she had actually encountered a soothsayer

Vincent Endwell

that had warned her away from the site. The day of the robbery, as she had been walking from the end of the bus line out of town, she and her buddy "Loon" Deleuze encountered a very pale woman all in black, standing on a plain stone pillar by an old well. Loon had almost said something snide about her when Tom stopped him, recalling a story her father had told her several years prior, in which a woman in black told her father not to visit his mother and spared him a horrible car accident.

Tom and Loon stopped before the woman, who let out a rolling pronouncement as they approached. I asked Tom to repeat what she said as close to verbatim as possible, and she recalled that the woman said, "There will be one who puts water on our tongues! It will come and quell the fire and place water on our thirsting tongues! But it is not the water of the swamp, it is not the water of the well! Keep your head clear of the drink of worms!"

While Tom's friend tugged at her arm, Tom asked the woman what she meant. But the woman all in black just stood silent, her face pointing up to the sky at a slight angle, mouth open, the way birds do in the heat. It was an uncanny sight, and Tom soon left. When the thefts began, she had a feeling deep in her gut that she needed to leave the job.

In her small half-painted home, I asked Tom if she ever got feelings like that again. She shrugged and passed me a pop from the fridge. "Sometimes," she said. For instance, she had a bad feeling about the wax museum before it burned down. But mostly she told me that it was just good, bog-standard common sense. "More people could do good with it, Hammond."

Problems at the Site Continue

George Wisniewski prides himself on being someone who doesn't let things go. In his off-hours, he was a coach for the Olyoke Middle School boys' soccer league for years even after his son graduated. He regarded himself as a good coach because of his tenacity; when there was a clear way one of his players needed to improve, he kept on coaching them until they grew as players. Some kids would join his team as shy and practically afraid of the ball; by the time he was through, they were some of his best pointers. That energy, he says, was shared with his work. When there was a problem, he wouldn't let it slide.

That hot 1973 summer, he really wished he could let his problems slide. It would have been a lot simpler, but when building materials kept going missing, he knew he didn't have long before the Grand Old-Tyme took notice. He hired men to set watches around the construction site at night, which was when the bulk of the thefts took place.

The daytime too was troubled. Wisniewski reckoned at this point he was losing about a man a week to heatstroke. While none buried themselves in the muck like they had the first day, he had to start keeping a man on shore to watch for others who collapsed into the water. It was through this practice that it was revealed that though some men collapsed, there was an equal number who spontaneously, voluntarily stuck their own faces into the muddy water.

When this occurred, they would be hauled out and brought to the office to cool. These men were always delirious, even while some appeared more lucid than others. The men who stuck their faces in were often more verbose, insisting that they were excruciatingly hot, as if they were burning up inside, and they needed water to cool them. All the men would say other strange things as well. Though they usually calmed after some hours in the cool air, they never acted quite the same even after recovering, and rarely stayed on the project. The look behind their eyes was haunted, as if they were always searching for something just out of sight.

Wisniewski tried to implement different working hours, ones that took the middle of the day off, but he started to receive pressure from the Grand Old-Tyme to keep construction at full pace. There was one particularly surreal argument with his manager over the phone. Wisniewski remembers his boss berating him in the middle of laying out his case, being told that the issue was overblown and that the workers were simply malingering. In the kitchen in the next room, a man was being held down by two others because he kept insisting that his head wasn't attached to his body, and had fallen off into his hands.

Nevertheless, construction continued apace. George Wisniewski knew things were getting dire; if he didn't find a solution soon, he was going to have a mutiny on his hands—or something worse.

An Incident at the Mountain Home

The owner of the Grand Old-Tyme was Orlie Trentham, familiar to those acquainted with town history as the television personality, owner of the local convenience store chain "Jumpin' Jacks," and a prominent member of the Church of the Revival. People had started flocking in droves to the Revival, and George Wisniewski remembers being irritated with Trentham for making it difficult to get his hands on his favorite Kentucky barrel-aged bourbon. At the time, he was made to cross state lines to get it, though he snorted while telling me "if he'd only known what was next."

Wisniewski interacted with Trentham very little, though. While he'd met the man when he was first hired for the job, and been impressed by his competence and unsettled by his character, he hadn't seen much of him since. Nevertheless, given the recalcitrance of his immediate supervisor, Wisniewski found himself hat-in-hand outside the Trentham home on Long End, ready to beg for a solution.

The Trentham mountain home was low, sprawling, and made of dark wood buried in trees and topiaries. At the time, the yard was well-maintained, and Wisniewski felt very out-of-place, ringing the doorbell among clipped hedges and roses. Inside, Mr. Trentham's house was full of oddities and curios that filled every available surface. Shelves were arranged with figurines, exotic and familiar, folk-quilting, clown masks, little icons of Mary, Joseph, and Jesus that had clearly been made by hand. Even the sofa where Wisniewski was instructed to sit barely had room for him amidst several porcelain dolls.

Perhaps most uncanny was the wax replica. Wisniewski recalls doing a double-take as he sat in that dim, expensive, cluttered living room. The life-size figure, standing in the light of the far window, was in fact a perfect wax sculpture of a young girl. She stood partly hidden by a grand piano, angled toward the green expanse of the backyard as if deep in contemplation, but wore a red party dress and Mary Janes of the sort a little girl might wear to a party in the sixties. It took Wisniewski many long moments of watching her before he was certain that she was just another piece of the collection, but even so he found his eyes drifting toward her, to check just one more time that she wasn't real.

Orlie Trentham himself, when he emerged from the darkened back half of the house, was very different than when George had seen him on television, or even when he'd been hired. Without the thick plaster of stage makeup sculpting his face, the man looked sickly and hollowed out.

"For a second," Wisniewski remarked to me, his eyes fixing on an indeterminate point, "I was so certain that he was completely empty. Like his skin was stretched over bones and stuffing and all that, but there was nothing deep inside his core. It was something about his cheeks, and how the inside of his mouth was kind of yellow when he talked. But like I was saying, that passed in a second. Just a crazy thought I could never get out of my head."

In the conversation that followed, George found himself briefly hopeful as he laid out his case. Orlie Trentham listened attentively right up until the end, when he shook his head. Georgie, he said, this is just the sort of thing that happens here.

"Georgie, you wouldn't want to make Orlie mad about this, would you? You wouldn't want to get him all fired up? There's a lot of people waiting on this project, Georgie. There's a lot of people who are asking Orlie *when's it going to be done, when are we able to get moving?* You wouldn't want to disappoint them either because you got spooked, would you?"

Staring into Mr. Trentham's sunken eyes, George Wisniewski was reminded of rumors he'd come across regarding what went on in the Church of the Revival, the infamous legends with which most everyone in Olyoke is familiar. It seemed to him as well, as Trentham explained the importance of the project and his visions for the park that would come to be called Hailey Land, and how grand and revitalizing it would be (recovering some of Mr. Trentham's bouncy, energized television personality), that Trentham referred to himself quite frequently in the third person. Indeed, as he got more showman-like, it seemed as if he was intentionally making his and Wisniewski's names rhyme like a song, drawing some strange symmetry between them.

Completely unsettled, sinking into that dusty living room sofa, Wisniewski felt a crushing, claustrophobic sense around him, an undeniable feeling that something wanted to drag him deep down, like a sucking, muddy pit opening beneath his feet. The collar of his shirt was soaked clean through, and sweat dripped down his face like rainwater. Orlie leaned in toward him, and seemed to tower over top as if Wisniewski were a child, then an ant, then a speck of dust gazing up at a colossus which rose taller than the clouds. He felt that he could not breathe, as if the air were clouded with dust, and he had a sudden strong knowledge that his soul was being winnowed away, as if he were on a tether that was being pulled far into some chasm of the world.

Gasping, George made excuses and hurried outside into the bleaching sun. The dark pall lessened as he left, as if he were scrambling his way out of a pit. As he glanced back, however, the dark house seemed to draw his eyes like marbles rolling down a hill, and he swore he saw Orlie standing in the shaded windows. His arm was around a small figure, as if a child had come up to watch George's shameful retreat.

Construction on the drain continued apace.

"Loon" Deleuze's account at the Jumpin' Jacks

The month was now August. Even working the night watch shift, Donald "Loon" Deleuze felt as if he were constantly swimming through steaming mud. Given the task along with Smith "Two Last Names" Jones of preventing materials theft from the site, Loon's shift started at sundown, right when Mr. Wisniewski was heading out.

Every evening, Loon recalls feeling a crushing dread as he left the house. Despite it still being light, the shadows seemed to get longer and longer every evening. Loon would take his route under the streetlights to the Jumpin' Jacks on the edge of town, and then the rest of the way there would be no streetlights at all.

By August, he had started lingering at the Jumpin' Jacks for his dinner, taking his time to order and glancing out the windows at the falling evening, imagining what might be out there in the dusk. Despite many nights on the job, Loon never felt comfortable at the site, and neither did Two Last Names. They would spend the hours from sundown to four a.m. nervously playing cards on the deck of the office, swatting away the clouds of bugs that bothered them, and doing rounds whenever it got too miserable to sit still. They were always covered in bug bites, and the night sounds were often uncanny. Along with the creak of crickets and the high singing of the red-frogs, there were other low thrumming sounds from out across the Splitridge Marsh. Almost on the edge of his hearing, the sounds seemed to resonate in Loon's bones more than his ears. Suffice to say, Loon and Two Last Names only ever did the rounds together, never alone.

Loon was fresh out of high school at the time, but had already made himself known to be a reliable worker. He described himself as a bit of a nerd, despite being a champion "lumberjacker"—the annual festival sport of log rolling, single buck, and pole climbing. He had won the Olyoke women's lumberjacking competition two times, once in 1970 and again in 1972. A hefty, muscled woman, Loon nevertheless wasn't much of a talker, and had spent the rest of his time in high school reading dime detective novels. With his mop of blond hair and uncertain face, it's not difficult to glimpse a more sensitive side beneath Loon's impressive size. Two Last Names would needle him about his nervousness, but Loon was certain that it was only to stop Two Last Names from feeling afraid himself.

"There was something wrong out on the water," Loon insisted. "I didn't want to believe it, but I could feel it in my gut. I really wish I'd listened to it."

One evening in August, as Loon was purchasing his hoagie at the sundown Jumpin' Jacks, that dread started eating at him again, like shadows were lingering and listening around him. He remembers standing by the deli counter, working up the courage to order, when he noticed someone in the next row over, staring at him over the shelves. He could only see out of the corner of his eye, but he was certain they were staring at him, unblinking, eyes fixed right on his face. His breath caught in his throat, and he badly wanted to glance over, but didn't want to be wrong, or worse, make eye-contact with someone he'd regret.

But the person didn't stop looking, even as he ordered his sandwich, and finally he could take it no longer. He whirled around, staring straight into the eye of a very strange woman, watching him from over the racks of honeybuns.

Vincent Endwell

She had hair the color of bleached hay: a rough, reedy mop that fell limply to either side of her head. Her cheeks were hollowed, and her eyes were sunken in her head, not quite filling out her eyelids. Her eyes themselves were a flat gray, as if she were blind, but she was staring straight at Loon. Prior to the draining, there were people who lived out on the marsh, and Loon wondered if possibly this woman was one of them. They had a strange reputation, although he wasn't sure he'd met any to say one way or the other.

Loon asked if she needed something, to which she replied, "There's not enough water." Confused, Loon pointed her to the spigot out front. As if exasperated, she continued to explain: "There's not *enough* water."

Disconcerted, Loon offered to show her if she liked. At this, she reached for his shoulder. He felt like he couldn't move away as she rested her hand on him. She was damp, and her hand was heavy and limp, as if there were no bones in it at all. As he gazed into her eyes, his neck at a strained angle, he was certain she was mouthing something at him.

He did not know what she said.

An Altercation

Two Last Names Jones was known around the site as a bit of a hothead. Wisniewski was aware of his reputation as a quick-tempered man, but Two Last Names was also a reliable worker and never missed a shift, and he figured that by pairing him with the even-keel Loon, he might balance the man out a bit.

For some weeks, this worked. That August night, however, Loon recalls getting into an argument with Two Last Names. After high school, Loon had ended up with Janie Duvall, a girl that Two Last Names had been on-again-off-again with for some years. Out in the circle of old orange light, some bad feelings came up once more like muck turning over, and a tenuous friendship broke apart again. Two Last Names accused him of stealing her; Loon recalls that he may have said some unpleasant things as well. Around two in the morning, Two Last Names shoved Loon back into his chair. While Loon reeled, Two Last Names took the flashlight and stomped off on the rounds.

Olyoke

This was the first time either of them had ever gone to do rounds by themselves.

The swamp sounds were louder than ever that night. Loon tapped his fingers waiting for Two Last Names to return, as the low hum out on the marshes grew ever more insistent, like water lapping at a levee. In the hanging vines and willows, Loon kept imagining that he could see things moving about in the brush.

Two Last Names had been gone for an hour, and Loon was considering leaving, no matter that he'd lose his job, when he heard running up the dirt road from the site. Two Last Names was panting, flashlight beam bobbing, and shouted, "I saw them, Loon! They're here! Come on! The worm people are here!"

That was when the flashlight beam flickered off. Two Last Names was still over fifty feet out. Loon grabbed his own flashlight, but it couldn't pierce the cloying, heavy darkness. Beyond the patch of light around the porch, Loon heard footsteps, and then the sound of something being dragged slowly toward the marsh.

Two Last Names had had the keys to the office, and so Loon was unable to get inside through the door. He eventually had to break and shimmy in a window to make a radio call, there being no landline in the temporary structure. It took him another hour to get through to anyone. When the sheriff arrived at dawn, he considered Loon's delay suspicious and took Loon into custody, though he was later released.

A search team headed by George Wisniewski set out at nine that morning, just as the heat was starting. Unusually, George remembers the red-frogs were still singing their nighttime song, as if they couldn't see that the sun was awake.

The body of Two Last Names Jones was found with an ax-cleft to the head by the mouth of an unknown path across the marsh. From the lack of blood spatters and marks in the dirt, it was clear he had been moved some ways—from almost back by the trailer. A n ax was found days later, in the marsh waters not too far from the office—an old woodcutter's ax.

Suspicion turned to Loon, former champion of the lumberjack games. Despite the circumstantial connection, however, and a possible motive, there were still unanswered questions: Why Loon would have been carrying such an ax on him, for instance, and where the missing materials were going. The ax itself was also not the sort used in lumberjack games—it was functional, and clearly hand-made, with a carved oak handle and a rough-pounded head.

One night shortly, George Wisniewski was woken to a phone call from the coroner, a friend of his. While his wife slept, the coroner told him that the cause of death had been drowning, not the ax wound. His lungs were full of water. When George asked why he was being informed of this, not being authorized by the police, the coroner paused for a long time.

"Because, George, I needed to talk to someone. His lungs are full of water, but he keeps yelling at me."

The Search Party

The next day, George Wisniewski and three others set off into the marsh. They didn't say as much outright, but they knew they needed to prove Loon Deleuze innocent. The three included Marcus Lawson, Hank Ogden, and Tom Halliday, who had been Loon's mentor.

They sought the path across the semi-drained marshland. Tom recalled thinking to herself that this was an awful idea, knowing the sort of things that happened to people out on the marsh, but knowing she couldn't let either Loon or George down. Beads of sweat formed along George's receding hairline and quickly soaked through his shirt. He brought with him a heavy flashlight, although the sun was high, and kept it braced on one shoulder.

Willows soon gave way to alders, tall reeds, and burn-vines. The path out was a narrow strip of dry land in between sucking mud, and they had to look closely not to misstep and fall into mud that would suck them down to their necks. George made sure to mark the path with ties as well. As the day grew long and hot, the sun a sickly red in the sky, thirst crept up on them. When George realized that Marcus had drunk almost all his water, he insisted they ration the rest. Tom understood why.

"It wasn't even dehydration he was worrying about," Tom said. "He was worried we'd run out of things to drink."

Tom could feel her thirst rising as they went further in, until even the murky water to either side of the path looked clear and refreshing. She bit her tongue between her teeth to keep herself from thinking about it.

Olyoke

Marcus Lawson was the one to break first. Ahead, a cool stream of water trickled down the path from around a turn in the alders, and Marcus made a run for it, trying to stick his face in it and lap it up. Tom and Hank got him after a few sips, and had to haul him away from it. George was insistent they turn back, but Hank had a hunch they were close.

Indeed, around the next turn, not even fifty feet away, rose a huge, twisted oak. Around the tree, as if forming a massive wasp's hive around it, were all the materials from the construction site. Boards, bricks, concrete, all wrapped around the oak like a nest, one that must have taken weeks and weeks and many hands to build. From beneath the mass of boards trickled cold, clear well water. Beside it all was a wooden hand-ax—stained brown with blood.

According to Tom Halliday, it was like something snapped in Mr. Wisniewski. As Tom and Hank tried to keep a hold of Marcus, George marched forward under the sweltering sun, grabbed the hand ax in a tight grip, and began swinging at the wasp's nest of boards around the tree. Marcus broke free and began to help, and then Tom and Hank glanced at each other and began to pull it apart as well, tearing off boards with just their bare hands.

When the oak was finally exposed, it was revealed to have a cleft in the trunk from where the spring water spilled. Not yet finished, George drove the ax into the cleft.

With a great, yawning, creak, the trunk began to split apart, as all that had been holding it together was the construction around it. The two halves of the tree hewed apart and fell in a leafy crash each to one side.

And remaining wedged into one of the sides, the tree's growth perfectly encompassing her, was a young girl, curled into a ball and fast asleep.

The Prophet Girl

As George pulled the girl out of the tree, a group of people emerged from the swampy overgrowth. They were pale and wore the handmade clothes of the swamp folk who rarely entered town. While the four investigators didn't know them, this was Ricky

Elder and his wife Yvonne, along with some others from the nearby village.

Ricky Elder is now in his late sixties, living in the same trailer he did then. He resides there with Yvonne and his three dogs: Lucky, Chowder, and Burger Boy. A broad man with shaggy white hair, he sports an assortment of tattoos and glasses the size of saucers, which he has worn since he was a child. He now works as a bartender at the Grisham Inn, though he intends to retire any day. That day, he recalls gathering people with urgency, as he learned of the group of construction workers headed toward the oak in the center of the swamp. It was important that they stop the group before their actions unknowingly led to disaster.

Some twenty years ago, Ricky explained, the ville, as they called it, had been visited by a prophet girl. Some in the ville thought she was the Trenthams' missing girl, but when asked, the girl denied it. She was no more than ten, and when she spoke she gave strange proclamations which often came true, and she vomited murky swamp water. Ricky had been a teen at the time and recalls the older people in the village remarking that she must have gained prophecy through a "trip to Blessed Well," which is a saying that refers to a particularly deep portion of the swamp that is rarely traveled—though no such location exists to Ricky's knowledge.

It was agreed, with the assent of the prophet girl, that the only way to free the girl from the weight of prophecy was to place her in the tree. The oak on the island, Ricky Elder explained, was hundreds of years old, and had a cleft in its trunk where such things could be placed until they were cured. This was one of many practices common to the ville, though Ricky has only observed it once.

Therefore the girl remained safely in the trunk, asleep, a dribble of water running still from her lips, where she was meant to remain until the curse was no longer. She remained there for nearly two decades, while the ville watched over her.

As the swamp began to be drained, however, the people of the ville realized that the tree was cracking open. Nervous that their home was to be destroyed, the people (including Ricky) stole materials from the construction site, which they used to protect the tree from cracking further. The ax had been found tossed amid a pallet of wood and nails that the people of the ville had stolen, and Ricky had left it for the rescuers to find in good faith. Ricky denied committing the murder and denied that anyone else in the ville had as well, which he expressed to Wisnewski and his crew.

So who then killed Two Last Names Jones?

The Aftermath

When I asked what George had thought when Ricky Elder spoke to him, he became quiet again.

"I didn't know what to do. I had this girl in my arms I'd pulled from a tree, and it all became kind of hazy at that point. Whatever was in the water, maybe. And I thought, God. I just don't know what the right thing here is." He was glad when the other construction workers spoke up and insisted the girl be returned to the swamp folk.

Upon returning to the construction site, axe in hand, George was greeted by a strange sight. Waiting for him were Trevor and "Holler" Trentham, Orlie Trentham's adult sons. Trevor was slender and very tall, while Holler was broad and even taller, with a remarkably large mouth. They insisted that they would take the axe to the police, and George got the sense that he couldn't refuse them. When the pair left, Tom Halliday recalls there was the strong scent of plain candle wax that hung cloyingly in the air.

The conclusion of the case was strange and messy.

When asked about the prophet girl, Ricky Elder was cagey. "You'll have to ask her yourself, if you can find her," he said. "She's a very, very private person."

Without the girl left to protect, the theft of materials at the site ceased. The draining of the swamp was completed officially in 1976, and the first Hailey Land attractions open to the public were the Rolling Stone Tilt-A-Whirl, Country Corral, and the Wax Museum in 1982.

Ricky Elder recalls the resignation of the ville as the tree's cracking completed, but also the reassurance from the older members of the community that there would be new growth. After a protracted legal battle, the theme park stopped just short of the ville, though current rumblings as of this writing indicate that the theme park board may want to expand further into the Splitridge region.

Wine and Crime Club—
Episode 121: A Cursed Play
and Quality Rosé

Intro music—
"Down in the Well" by Mother's Gone
When were you gonna call us home?
Cut my finger down to the bone?

IRVING: Welcome to the Wine and Crime Club, I'm Irving Bianchi—

JESSLYN: And I'm Jesslyn Campbell.

IRVING: And we're so happy to be recording live with you all today here in the historic Lenore Theater, in beautiful Olyoke, Tennessee. Thanks so much for having us, y'all.

AUDIENCE APPLAUDS AND CHEERS.

OLYOKE

IRVING: We've got a story for you tonight that we think y'all will like, and probably a handful of our local listeners will be familiar with. For anyone tuning in for the first time, we like to do local stories on live shows, and so this one was selected from a number of tales people sent after we announced the tour locations. And can I say, you all had some *good* ones.

JESSLYN: Truly.

IRVING: Olyoke is a busy town.

JESSLYN: I wanted to do the one about the murders at Hailey Land—which, for those who don't know, is Hailey Temple's theme park—but Irving nixed it.

IRVING: I didn't *nix* it, I just thought this story would be a better fit, considering that we're recording *in the theater where part of it happened*.

JESSLYN: Are you going to tell them what our story is?

IRVING: Yes, but first tell me what you're drinking today.

JESSLYN: [laughs] Malt water.

IRVING: Ooh, deviating from the rosé, I see.

JESSLYN: Well, when in Rome. It's quite good. [JESSLYN offers IRVING a sip.] Not quite what you expect, is it?

IRVING: No, it's rather different. It's kind of savory?

JESSLYN: Yeah, and a little sweet. What are you having?

IRVING: Does it matter?

JESSLYN: Yes, obviously.

IRVING: [sheepishly] Franzia.

JESSLYN: You Philistine.

IRVING: You can't talk, you drank rosé for ten straight episodes!

JESSLYN: Yes, but it was *quality* rosé.

IRVING: Audience, I need you to back me up here. Is it possible to have "quality rosé"?

AUDIENCE CHEERS AND BOOS SIMULTANEOUSLY.

JESSLYN: I think the vote is split. [Takes a sip of malt water.] Okay, so let's get into the episode. What are you telling me about today?

IRVING: Right, so today's story requires a little set-up. In the original email I got about this, one of our listeners told us to look into something they called the "cursed last play of Jeremy Ries."

JESSLYN: Already a great start.

IRVING: Right? It's a play titled *A Pyramid Fit for a King*, and it was the last composition of local playwright and poet Jeremy Ries before his disappearance—ruled a death—in 1962.

JESSLYN: Ooooh.

IRVING: Jeremy Ries was born in 1929 and did most of his writing in the fifties. He's pretty obscure today, but he was locally acclaimed at the time. His shows were produced by some big-name companies, including the Silver Dollar Theater Troupe and the Center for the Arts in Nashville. But yeah, today people mostly remember him for *A Pyramid*.

JESSLYN: Interesting . . . Why is the play cursed? Or why do people say it is?

IRVING: Well, there's a lot of reasons. [laughs] To start, it was only ever officially performed once, though maybe twice unofficially.

JESSLYN: Weird.

IRVING: The first performance was strange enough to give the play part of its cursed reputation, or at least make people believe that bad things would happen if it was performed. It was actually performed here, in the Lenore Theater, in 1966, by the Worthy Crafts Theater Company. It was supposed to be the flagship performance of their season of shows, but from the start things got a little weird.

JESSLYN: How so?

IRVING: Most of what I could find was from

two sources. One was the original newspaper review after the show, which people have preserved, and the other was an article written years later. It seems like the director stopped leaving the theater for a few weeks prior to the show being put on. People thought he was just really dedicated, but one of the crew spoke to him about it, and he said with real weariness, "Oh, do the doors exist for you?"

JESSLYN: [sips drink] Well that's bizarre. So it seems like maybe he *couldn't* leave? Or didn't think he could?

IRVING: [pointing backstage] Evidently he set up a cot in one of the dressing rooms back there, which we were investigating before the show started, and used the bathroom and hose in the basement to keep clean. People brought food to the rehearsals, and so he lived like that for *weeks*.

JESSLYN: Do you think the Lenore Theater will let us go look in the basement after this?

IRVING: [laughs] I mean, they already were pretty generous by letting us poke around the upstairs.

JESSLYN: [speaking to someone in the tech booth] Hey Steve, will you show us the basement after this?

OLYOKE

DISTANT WORDS ARE SPOKEN, NOT MIC'ED.

JESSLYN: He's saying maybe. Thanks Steve, we'll stop bothering you now.

AUDIENCE LAUGHTER.

JESSLYN: So this director. He had to be pretty concerned about what would happen to him when the play was over.

IRVING: Yeah, one would guess. But no one ever really got to ask him about it.

JESSLYN: That doesn't sound promising.

IRVING: Right. The performance itself goes very weird. Firstly, the play is very strange. I'm going to get into what's actually in it next, but it was apparently nothing like Ries had ever written. It's a meandering story, barely has a plot, and is full of soliloquies by the three main characters, who keep referencing other events and people that aren't explained. It ends gruesomely, too. So the audience was already extremely weirded out by the production. But what really freaked them out was when it . . . started over.

Vincent Endwell

JESSLYN: Like the next night?

IRVING: No. Immediately after. The final lines were said, but the actors never bowed. They just started again with the first scene. They performed for *over 14 hours* before people finally pulled them off the stage. And when asked why they had done so, the actors all expressed that they believed something to be watching the performance, and, "If we don't stop, it won't come."

JESSLYN: Uhhh. That's creepy as hell. Why didn't anyone pull them off the stage sooner?

IRVING: Maybe when the performance kept going on, everyone went home, and it was only the following morning that enough people thought to do something about it? Or maybe they were up all night talking and trying to figure out what to do. I'm not sure.

JESSLYN: Hmm. Also, what did they say? "If we don't stop, it won't come"? What's that supposed to mean?

IRVING: Well, I don't know for sure. They said the director had been telling them of something called the "headless giant," that would arrive when the play was over. And maybe it did, because after the play had ended, the director vanished. No one saw him leave the building, but he wasn't in the back of the theater or at his home. Maybe he packed up and ran before anyone could question him. But it's a real mystery. He must have fled town, because as far as I could tell, no one saw him again.

OLYOKE

I even looked for death records for a while, and never found them.

JESSLYN: That's extremely bizarre. So no one ever performed the play after that again, I'm assuming?

IRVING: It was pretty frowned upon, and there are barely any copies of it remaining. It's also just not that entertaining a play to perform, I've heard, so that's not helping. But actually, there are rumors that *A Pyramid* was related to the performance put on by a community theater director here in Olyoke in 2003 at a town celebration.

The play that was produced was an original composition by her, but evidently some of the lines sounded very similar to *A Pyramid*, and the play was . . . well . . . In a really gruesome twist, the theater director actually killed her ex-husband on stage as part of the show.

JESSLYN: What the *fuck*, that's horrible.

IRVING: Yeah, it's really grim. There's something really fucked up about this play. From some of the things the director said, it sounded as if she had realized something profound that led to her killing her husband—that he wasn't real, and that something else was coming.

JESSLYN: Maybe the play compels you to do horrible things?

IRVING: Maybe. But to me, it seems like it makes you *realize* something so horrible that you have no choice but to do something horrible to prevent it.

JESSLYN: I don't like that, that's very creepy.

IRVING: Yeah. And I gotta be honest, looking into the playwright himself doesn't make me feel any better about that.

JESSLYN: Right, so what's up with that guy?

IRVING: So I mentioned already that he disappeared in 1962, and it was later ruled a murder.

JESSLYN: Wait, murder? You said death.

IRVING: Oh, did I? Yeah, his disappearance was ruled a murder.

JESSLYN: Did they ever find the body?

IRVING: No. But it was in part because of this play that law enforcement was actually able to prosecute someone for his murder.

JESSLYN: How is that possible?

IRVING: This play was discovered posthumously. But it was discovered posthumously in the belongings of someone who was in the same artist's society as Jeremy Ries—called the Society of Pursuivant Nazarenes. They were known for some strange beliefs and characters. Another one of the members was Hieronymus Johnson, who is the architect of a number of buildings in town, including this theater.

AUDIENCE MEMBER: [distantly] And 'Spirition!

IRVING: The reason why law enforcement even found the play is because another member of this society, Colonel Carson Langley, was arrested on suspicion of starting the *fire* at the mill studio of Hieronymus Johnson, which led to Johnson's death and the destruction of much of his work and writings.

AUDIENCE MEMBER: [distantly] Don't forget 'Spirition!

IRVING: Sorry, I can't make out what you're saying out there. Can you hold that until the Q&A at the end? Thanks, dude.

JESSLYN: Wait, so, they believed strange things. Similar to what the play makes people believe? Elaborate on that. Just what is this group? The Society of . . .

IRVING: Pursuivant Nazarenes.

JESSLYN: I don't even know what that means.

IRVING: Pursuivant means like, a follower, or attendant. It's archaic.

JESSLYN: So they were like, following God?

IRVING: Maybe? Most of what is known about them comes largely from Hieronymus Johnson, who wrote a number of essays and journals about his beliefs about the world and his architecture. He designed buildings around the notion that something, some kind of cataclysm, was going to arrive, and he needed to make a structure that would allow people to escape. He saw himself as kind of a Noah figure, building an ark to survive the flood.

JESSLYN: Through architecture?

IRVING: So what's funny is that Ries's work

also talks a lot about a cataclysm that's coming, though more obliquely because his works were fictional. This seems to be a unifying belief of the people of the Society, that some cataclysm was coming. For Johnson, his writings talk about trying to build toward a spiritual "second layer" that would be above whatever catastrophe was going to arrive. His buildings, either literally or through some kind of special geometry, were supposed to allow one to ascend above the cataclysm.

In some of his writings, he also contrasts this with another view which he attributes to "the Colonel," which is that the cataclysm will come at the end of an event, or performance, or celebration. It wasn't clear if this performance was a particular one to bring about the cataclysm, or if it was a warning that the cataclysm would arrive when an event was through.

JESSLYN: Hmm . . . Okay, so maybe these people are a little unhinged? That's sort of the vibe I'm getting.

IRVING: They definitely had some odd beliefs, I'll give you that.

JESSLYN: I would love to know how they found each other.

IRVING: Maybe they put out an ad.

JESSLYN: "Want to join our murder and fire club? We have endless plays, fucked up buildings, and booze! Join here!"

IRVING: You joke, but people also listen to our podcast.

JESSLYN: [considering] You know what? Valid.

IRVING: I will admit to being intrigued by the notion of something catastrophic happening because someone held a performance. Like those actors performing A *Pyramid*, or like that theater director. It does kind of make you wonder if it's just performing the play, or if it could be any play, or any event. Like, what if it could be any performance put on in a building built by Johnson?

JESSLYN: Like this one, you mean.

IRVING: Well, I don't know that this is a performance.

JESSLYN: I don't know what else you call it.

IRVING: A podcast taping.

JESSLYN: Yeah, but it's also a performance. Like, I wouldn't say I'm fake on the podcast, but I'm also not 100% my authentic self. There is a performance happening, because there's an audience (hi guys) and that's the nature of the show.

IRVING: I guess so.

JESSLYN: Yeah.

IRVING: That's not very comforting.

JESSLYN: Yeah, I don't love that.

IRVING: Hm. Anyway . . . Bringing us back, basically what happened in 1964 is that Hieronymus Johnson was killed in a fire, Colonel Carson Langley was linked to the scene by witnesses, he was arrested, and then they found a lost play of Jeremy Ries in his home. Which brings us to what was actually in *A Pyramid Fit for a King* that was compelling enough to make people think that Colonel Carson Langley murdered Jeremy Ries.

JESSLYN: Right. Do we have that? Didn't you say copies of the play are super rare?

IRVING: [rustling of folded paper] Well, do I have a surprise for you.

[JESSLYN squeals]

IRVING: A contact of mine hooked us up. This came from a Xerox of a retyped version of the first printing that evidently lives at a historical society somewhere. But it's legit, I read through it. And Jesslyn? It's fascinating.

JESSLYN: I'm on the edge of my seat, this isn't real. This is great. Real quick, are we going to get cursed?

IRVING: Honestly, even if it weren't too long to read it all aloud, I don't think I would for that reason. Better not to risk it. I'm just going to describe what's in it, and read one or two excerpts.

JESSLYN: So we'll only get a little cursed.

IRVING: Yeah, I think that should be a fine level of curse. Let me know if you start believing in an earth-shaking catastrophe.

JESSLYN: [takes another sip of malt water] Okay, so what's in this thing?

IRVING: Right, so *A Pyramid Fit for a King*

has three main characters, who are called the Herald, the Lion, and the Poet. Our main character, if you will, is the Herald, who wakes up at the start of the play. The Herald is called "it" throughout the play, which is interesting, I'm not sure why. It wakes up at the start and begins looking for someone called the Poet. Some people have said it's implied that the Herald seems to be waking up from being drugged. The Herald does open by lamenting,

"He said he wouldn't do it. Why did I believe him? I am so *gullible*. *We* are all so gullible."

EMPTY SILENCE (~5 SECONDS).

JESSLYN: Okay. And you mentioned that this play depicts something in real life, so are all the characters supposed to be someone real?

IRVING: There are some parallels, but it's hard to say. It's rumored that the Herald might be a Society member known as E. Haskill, who also became inactive around the same time that Ries disappeared, but that's a little murky because E. Haskill was a pseudonym, and there's no consensus on who it referred to.

JESSLYN: Gotcha.

Vincent Endwell

IRVING: So, the first section of the play involves the Herald looking around a festival, talking to people and inquiring about the location of the Poet. The people it talks to are all in masks, and are almost comically unhelpful—they describe their own personal problems at great length, and the Herald seems unable to simply leave these conversations. The Herald itself is in a sort of black bird costume, and is described as wearing a bird mask. There's a refrain that's repeated through this part: all the partiers end their conversations by asking the Herald when the celebration is going to begin, and the Herald has to keep saying that it doesn't know, no one told it.

This sequence seems like it takes probably over thirty minutes, judging by the amount of text.

JESSLYN: Uhh. Interesting.

IRVING: [flipping through pages] But finally the Herald is followed by a spotlight, and the crowd moves offstage, and it finds the characters of the Lion and the Poet. At first, we just hear their voices bickering with each other. The Lion keeps telling the Poet to stay still with this sort of menacing affection, and the Poet keeps going on about how he hopes a piece that he's written will be acclaimed.

The spotlight swings to the front of the stage, and as the Herald approaches it, the stage floods with light. The Lion is dressed all in white, and the Poet is dressed like a red lion with a yarn mane, which isn't confusing at all. And the Lion is currently sealing up the Poet inside of a wall with plaster.

JESSLYN: Oh god.

IRVING: Much of the rest of the play is the Herald, the Lion, and the Poet arguing with each other cryptically, while the Poet is half in and out of this wall. The Herald is convinced the Lion has betrayed some group of people, which includes the Poet, while the Lion tries to convince it that being sealed in the wall is the way to avoid the cataclysm that is coming, and that because of this, the Poet will be resurrected after the cataclysm.

Throughout, there are a number of stage directions for a "rattling and rumbling" that is supposed to emanate from somewhere. I'm not sure what it's supposed to be—maybe that was envisioned to be something done with drums.

Finally, though, the Herald goes to pull the Poet from the wall, and the Lion kills it with a knife. The end heavily implies that the Lion seals both the Poet and the Herald inside of the wall with the plaster.

EXTENDED PAUSE (~8 SECONDS)

JESSLYN: Damn, alright. I have a lot of questions. I guess my first is, is the Poet supposed to represent Jeremy Ries?

IRVING: That's the most common interpretation. Ries was a poet as well as a playwright, and the character seems to be a caricature of him. Those who knew him recognized his general optimistic attitude, though here it's taken to a bizarre extreme.

JESSLYN: And the Lion is supposed to be, what was his name, Colonel Langley.

IRVING: Right.

JESSLYN: Strange. So the main draw of this play is what people think it means about how Ries and Haskill were killed. Is there really evidence to believe that's the case, and this isn't just, I don't know, weird fanfiction?

IRVING: There's a few reasons. One, the way the Lion is written about in the play is really interesting. The stage directions treat him with almost glowing esteem. At one point, he's described as mockingly wiping an imaginary tear from beneath the Herald's eye, and the stage directions say that this "demonstrates his great sympathy and compassion." Or the stage directions will assume something about what the audience is feeling. Another time—let me just read this.

"THE LION stops and turns with his hands on THE HERALD's shoulders. His magnificent and commanding presence makes THE HERALD appear to be realistically small and frail, much to the pity of the audience. THE HERALD's back is to THE POET, and scraping continues outside of the light."

SILENCE (10s)

JESSLYN: Weird. So, people could believe that Colonel Langley was pretty vain and would write this weird, self-aggrandizing play about himself.

IRVING: Ha, yeah. There's this weird tension in it, where the Herald kind of acts as our main character, but when the Lion shows up, it's like he's inserting himself as the hero, despite the fact that he's shown to be a murderer.

JESSLYN: But . . . I still don't get how this is evidence. It wasn't like they ever found Jeremy Ries or this E. Haskill walled up in the plaster somewhere, was it?

IRVING: To be honest, I think the main evidence was that the colonel was caught red-handed setting a lethal fire. But that is the other circumstantial evidence—the year that Jeremy Ries went missing was the same year that Hieronymus Johnson's mill studio was built. So the thought was that not only might Colonel Langley have sealed Ries and Haskill into the walls as it was being built, but that years later he chose that as the site to kill Johnson to get rid of the evidence.

JESSLYN: So did they find the bodies in the wreckage?

IRVING: Well, no.

JESSLYN: There's no way it burned hot enough to destroy them, right?

IRVING: I couldn't say, but that does seem unlikely. So it seems more than possible that this play doesn't actually depict what happened to Ries—or if it does, it wasn't at the mill studio. There was a lot of construction at the time—the theater was also going up, so frankly, it could be in this building.

JESSLYN: Oh *boy*. That's terrifying.

IRVING: But probably not. I think if you sealed a body in plaster, it wouldn't keep its integrity for long.

JESSLYN: No, yeah, probably not.

IRVING: But yeah, that's the story of *A Pyramid Fit for a King*, and the alleged murder of Jeremy Ries. A series of very strange events, without any real answers. I guess our little epilogue is that Colonel Langley was jailed, and passed away in the 90s. Also, the world hasn't ended yet.

JESSLYN: Dang, that was a great one. I'm going to be thinking about that for a while. The weird ones always get me. Like— give me a good slasher story over this. Ha—I almost don't want to end the show.

IRVING: [laughing uncomfortably] Me

neither. It wasn't getting to me before, but right now, looking around at all the detailing in this old theater, the fact that the audience is just a black blob . . . Hey guys . . .

JESSLYN: Should we do some Q&As? Turn on the houselights and all that?

IRVING: Yeah, yeah. Let's do that. We'll end the podcast recording here, though, so this will be what goes up on the feed.

JESSLYN: Perf. Thanks for joining us, you bunch of winos. [clink of glass as the hosts toast one another] Cheers.

Outro music:
"Down in the Well" by Mother's Gone
Why couldn't you dream yourself free?
Why wouldn't you stay here with me?
Ring of light from the tomb of the well
Living in our own little hell
Living in our own little hell

The Strange Case Of The Collapsible Man

The thunderstorm came in a deluge with no warning, and it was just Leah and the well-dressed man at the bus depot, no one else to fill the hard plastic seats so lovingly bolted to the floor. They were both positioned so that they could keep an eye on the unchanging departure screen as the rain smeared against the windows.

Leah couldn't quite remember why they had started talking. Oh, no, she did—it was just a little thing. The well-dressed man had asked her if she had a charger. She had, and offered it to him, and he stood with his phone plugged in at the outlet near her, politely not making eye contact. She had a suspicion that if it had been the other way around, her asking him for a charger, he wouldn't have even responded to the request, let alone an attempt at conversation. But something about him being forced to debase himself by asking for a simple favor had broken some kind of wall, and when she asked him where he was going, he answered.

"Back home. Chattanooga," he said, all staccato. "Yourself?"

And Leah had told him she was coming back from visiting relatives, but had class on Monday. They talked a little about her major at TSU: archaeology, coursework, this and that. The man was on the shorter side, with oiled dark hair, and that suit with the unique cufflinks and lapel pins like he had received some award. He didn't seem accustomed to being friendly. He spoke in short sentences, elaboration always tacked on as an afterthought and nothing more, information doled out like someone reluctant to share their candy. But he wasn't unpleasant, though Leah had certainly been a little intimidated when he first approached. There was a blunt, vaguely anxious man beneath the stormy exterior.

OLYOKE

When she asked him what he did, he was cagey. Something about acquisitions, but Leah didn't think he meant "mergers &." When asked what he was coming back from, he said with some hesitation, "From business. A business trip."

"What kind of business?" asked Leah, as the rain worsened outside with dispassionate catastrophe.

"You said you were an archaeology major. Is that right?" the man said, with an appraising jeweler's eye. "Well. I suppose this might interest you."

The woman's father had been a collector of strange and obscure items—Egyptian, Etruscan, Viennan, Ottoman. Museum quality artifacts. In his old age, her father had built a strange house for himself, a habitat somewhere between an A-frame and a pyramid hoisted on many stilts in the Alabaman wetlands. The interior was an amalgam of a hunting lodge and an Egyptian tomb: paintings of camouflaged deer hung beside pillars and obelisks, hieroglyphics and reliefs of the Nile pressed into the mantelpiece. A shower curtain printed with game birds opened to reveal a soap dish shaped like Nefertiti's head. The main room of the house was for his artifacts, and priceless vases and stonework sat protected beside stuffed animal heads, all before a brick fireplace and tall, thin windows.

His daughter hadn't known about his collection until he died. It seemed that perhaps she had not visited much. When he did, she found she had quite a difficult job on her hands selling it all. Much was quite valuable; some was not. Telling which was which was more work than she had wanted to put up with. She put it all into the hands of a society to deal with (and it was implied, Leah thought, that the well-dressed man belonged to this society), and the society would take a cut and the artifacts and she would walk away unburdened and a little richer. Well, simple enough. But that was before they knew about the collapsible man.

Leah had many questions, but she sensed that if she asked them all at once, she would frighten him off. She did try to make herself look as professional as possible while wearing a t-shirt with a cartoon dog on it. She thought she gave it a good effort. "The collapsible man," she repeated, curiosity boiling up like a mudspring. "I don't know what that is."

The collapsible man, he said. It seemed to be part of the collection, but the society wasn't sure from whence it came. It was old; its skin was leather, cracking and needing oils, and its joints squealed as it moved. Its garb was vaguely Thracian, with bag-like striped pants and a black tunic, and the distinctive alopekis, which Leah knew to be a foxskin hat with ears still visible. The eyes were polished stone. Its limbs were the most notable feature: long and variable in that length, they collapsed and extended from some unknown internal mechanism.

They had first thought to look for the collapsible man when they examined the artifact room and found a place labeled for him among the curios, but they had found nothing in the house. That first day, they had catalogued and moved the artifacts out to a rented truck, where they left them for the night. The second day, they found everything moved back to its place in the house, neatly arranged as if it had never been touched.

It seemed likely that the daughter must have known about the collapsible man. While he hated the wink of a camera and eschewed the scrutiny of multiple eyes, he did not remain entirely out-of-sight. In the corners of eyes he was glimpsed emerging from his hiding spaces within the walls, limbs unfolding wooden joint after wooden joint from the little places he had stashed himself. He was seen navigating the upstairs hallway, and stepping into the ventilation above the shower with a creak and a clack. Once, a long wooden pole was seen stretching across a room, only for it to be swiftly folded away and the watcher to realize that it was indeed one very, very long arm.

He did not respond at first to calls or questions, no matter how polite. His sole concern appeared to be that the old man's collection did not wander far from the house.

He was a curiosity to the society. In many ways, he seemed to be the most priceless artifact himself, albeit one difficult to date. Was he from Thrace? Was he merely dressed as such? Perhaps he was completely automatic like the promise of the Mechanical Turk, wound up and enacting the stuff of life without any internal knowledge of this fact. Given his fixation on the artifacts, there came the question: Was he alive, or was he merely following the orders of his mechanism?

The primary investigation was carried out by a colleague of the well-dressed man, while the others of his society sat blindfolded in the room one-over, taking detailed typewritten notes. In this way, they enticed the collapsible man to emerge for an extended session, filling only one orbit of the society man's vision, and he therefore managed to undertake a strange interview.

The collapsible man answered only with a turn or nod of his red-haired head. He was old; he didn't know if he was ancient, or perhaps did not care. He had been made; by whom, he didn't say. It was also unclear from where the old man had acquired him, or even if he had. The only statement to which the collapsible man would agree was that he had been made by an inventor, many years ago, and he had been designed for the purpose of lasting the ages.

How he had come to this house with the old man seemed to be irrelevant, or unknown. When asked what he thought of various parties—the old man, the daughter, the society—the collapsible man had little opinion. Any attempt to ask for an opinion, feeling, or expression of an internal state was also met with neutrality.

Indeed, the only firm conclusion that could be drawn from him was whether the artifacts could be removed from the house for sale. The answer to that was no, no, no. Nothing must ever change. Things had already changed enough.

The last question that was asked was how far the collapsible man could expand. As the interview drew to a close, the collapsible man's limbs grew longer and longer. They reached the walls and doubled back, then extended further. They filled the room, stretched through the hallways until the men of the Society feared that they would be unable to exit. They hurried out, tearing off their blindfolds, as the house behind them filled with long, leathery limbs. As the last man stepped outside, the door - now cross-hatched with limbs - shut behind them.

The society was faced with a conundrum. They had promised to deal with the artifacts for the daughter, and yet could not take them without upsetting the collapsible man. Yet it still remained unclear whether the collapsible man was sentient, or some kind of mechanized protector, wound up and set loose. They had many discussions about this, said the well-dressed man, and Leah imagined a conference of identical black-suited men around a table, their strange cufflinks all winking in a dim yellow light. They bore some amount of sympathy for the man, aware or not. They, too, protected a collection and wished for it to abide the sands of time. It was the natural condition of all beings to resist being scathed by the wearing edge of the ages.

Ultimately, though, they decided on a course of action. They could not outrun the grasp of the collapsible man. His reach was vast, maybe infinite. But he could also collapse, couldn't he? He could become quite small indeed. If some arrangement could not be made, if he could not be reasoned with . . .

As the well-dressed man said this, the rain let up slightly, and an announcement cut tinnily from the speakers that the buses, so delayed, were now approaching the station. Headlights cut through the four P.M. haze, but while Leah hurried to pack up her belongings, she tried to ask the well-dressed man what exactly the plan was.

The man returned her phone charger to her, and with a meaningful look he hoisted his luggage, which Leah realized now was more of a carrying case, made of black leather and sturdy steel reinforcements. And there was no time to ask what was in it, or why it shifted so strangely as he heaved it over his shoulder, because then the buses were loading up and the drivers were asking for tickets, and somewhere in the shuffle the well-dressed man got on one bus and Leah got on the other, wedged among many sleeping passengers.

And so that was that.

Itch

"It's not as bad when I'm at home. Mostly because I'm not around people."

Her therapist lifts his veil to take a sip of water. The fabric scrapes against his beard.

Doggedly, she continues. "I, uh. I can't stop thinking that I touched something, or brushed up against something, or just—got it on my skin somehow. And that makes me want to take off my gloves and scratch until it's out of my skin, which is crazy."

"Do you?" he asks. "Scratch?"

Her attention follows the glass as he sets it down, and she imagines everything that might have touched it before it got to his lips. A stray finger. The edge of the door handle as he entered. She imagines touching it in perverse defiance, smearing finger oil around the rim, and the screw's spiral wedge turns another notch in her mind. Her fingers tighten in her lap.

"Well, not in the moment," she says. "I sort of—save it up, until I'm completely sure there's nothing on my hands or anything left to touch. I, like—well, I mean, this sounds nuts, but I get home and strip off my gloves and my clothes, and leave them all in the laundry room, and I wash my hands in the laundry sink, and then I go into the bathroom, shower, and then I . . . scratch."

"Everywhere?"

"I mean, more or less," she says. Heat rises to her head, and for a moment, she can almost imagine she's caught the reem. The characteristic mild fever, followed by hives at the point of contact. Skin, but more often eyes are the point of transmission. Mucous membranes let the bacteria in. After, the rash spreads, the fever rises, the aches and chills start, the skin swells. Bloats. "Everywhere the bacteria might have got in."

"For example?" he asks. "I mean, do you scratch at your hands, your arms . . . ? I know you've mentioned the skin picking before around your fingers, but it sounds like this is more widespread—"

"I mean *everywhere*," she says, then quiets. "I mean, mostly hands and arms, under my nails, at my scalp, around my mouth, around my eyes—"

Up close to the mirror, cold porcelain sink pressed up against her stomach, she examines her eye. The skin has started to heal since yesterday, and she knows she should just not touch it. Just leave it alone. Stop looking altogether. But there's something about it, something about that little wet orb sitting in an orifice of viscous goo that makes her need to just—clean it out.

Mostly, it is the little blob of black jelly in the corner, stained from faded eyeshadow. Now that her hands are washed and scrubbed, she cleans it out with a nail and washes it down the drain. She shouldn't. She knows there could still be contamination beneath the nails, ground into the dead skin and dirt, but she does anyway. The tear ducts gleam livid pink to match the abrasion along the edge of her lower lid. It really is doing better, but there's just that little bit of dry skin, peeling off like parchment paper. Removing dead skin is good. Removing dead skin lets the healthy pink skin come through.

She knows this is wrong. She peels it off anyway. Her eyelid stings, and then settles into a low throb. The smallest welling of red blood presents itself like a cleansing font.

"The worst part is that this has made me a bad person," she says, her veil swaying slightly with her breath, brushing against her lips. "I just—I feel like I'm getting so judgmental and secretive. I'm taking every precaution, I'm being so careful, I'm not going around people except for these appointments and groceries, and the drugstore . . ." She twists her gloved hands in her lap. "Like, that's reasonable, right? I have to get soap, I have to get toothpaste, but even that I'm hesitant to tell people. What if I'm not being careful enough?"

"You sound like you're being careful enough," he says. His voice is calming, reassuring, but she isn't sure if she trusts his guidance anymore. He hasn't even sealed up his house—she knows, because a few weeks ago she drove by and saw the windows weren't saran-wrapped, and there were no cloths under the door. Red-frogs littered his lawn like autumn leaves, meaning they were close enough to crawl through some tiny gap. "Maybe you should consider seeing some friends. From a distance, in an area away from the water, of course, but just to talk."

"But that's what I'm *telling* you," she says, trying to keep her exasperation out of her voice. She now knows her feelings are justified—isn't it one of the worst things you can do, to be outside? Isn't that where it's most contaminated? But she doesn't want to argue. "I'm scared to. That's the other half of it. I don't want to get sick, but I also don't want to talk to anyone. What if they're not doing enough, and now I'm in danger? What if *I'm* not doing enough? What if they think I'm doing *too* much, or they try to tell me I am?"

Her therapist is silent for a moment. She wishes she could tell what he was thinking. Whether he's judging her, whether he really thinks she's nuts. She knows professional etiquette would forestall that, that it's sort of beside the point, but she worries. She wishes she were doing something else. She wishes she could literally tie her hands together to stop this need for awful itching, fidgeting movement.

"You're sure it's not because of the scratching?" he says. "You said it was pretty dramatic. I mean, I wouldn't know unless you'd told me, but I'm wondering if the compulsion is what's stopping you from going out."

She is so glad she's paying ninety bucks an hour for big insights like that. "Also that, I guess."

Outside, the frogs sing their maddening song. She puts on coffee to calm her nerves, less for any chemical benefit and more for the ritual of it. Can't think when your hands are busy. Beyond the window, the red-frogs hop by the edge of the water. They burrow their inflamed-red, pus-yellow bodies into the mud, leaving only their heads and their big scarlet mouths visible, open and singing.

It's a long, warbling, tuneless song—an endless round sung by a choir whose audience has left. It's crazy to think that before all this, she used to *like* the sound. Red-frogs had been an Olyoke thing, like malt water and burn-chicken. Now she would kill them all if she could, scorch the earth with fire if it meant they'd all die. She tries not to think about how one died on the walk and she stepped in it, its stomach-tongue shooting out of its spotted body like a gag gift, guts and blood staining her trainers. She tries not to think of the contamination in the sink, in the washer, in the trash bag, all the points of contact, all the ways it could get inside.

Making coffee. She's making her coffee. Water goes in the back. Filter goes in the bucket. Coffee grounds, thick and earthy, go in the filter. Most people don't get the reem from the frogs but from other people, once it has mutated through a human body to be even more transmissible and even more friendly to human skin. She saw a man at the grocery store with a rash on the back of his neck, and he wasn't touching it but he was touching things and putting them down, picking them up and putting them down, as if trying to put his mark on them. She left, she left immediately, but she had touched other things, too. She'd been wearing gloves, at least, but it was all she could think about.

Coffee starts bubbling, percolating. The sound reminds her of the frogs at the edge of the water, burrowing in and bubbling up. They live in the soil, sometimes waiting up to thirty years before emerging. Scientists on the radio have been talking about how there's actually another life phase, about how their metamorphosis is unique in that they have *three* stages post-egg. They hatch into a worm-like polyp, strangely enough, before becoming the usual wriggling, motile tadpole and then the frog. With each step the frogs turn more and more livid and crimson as bacteria accumulate in their skin and sac.

She has to shut it off before the segment finishes. She can't hear any more about them.

OLYOKE

As the coffee brews, a frog splats against the window. She flinches like she's been struck, nearly dropping her empty mug. The frog just sits there, stuck to the glass, yellow eyes bugging out at her like a fungal growth. The pink-orange sac bulges in its throat, carrying the bacterial slurry that makes them so deadly. It's like it's mocking her, daring her to go out there and kill it and seal her own doom. She tries not to look at it, focus on the coffee that's burbling, black and healthy, in the pot. Against the white counter, her hands are a score of torn pink lines, cracked and raw at the knuckles.

The peeling on her knuckles makes her think about her eyes, sitting in her head like bulbous little sacs. The frog's eyes roll and loll deliriously like an invalid. She knows she shouldn't touch her eyes with unclean hands, but she's been so good. She's cleaned everything in her house, bleached and sterilized every surface. She's scrubbed her hands. But still. Something might have gotten in, like how that frog is trying to get in, looking at her like a threat. She can't wash her hands again, though. It's too painful. They're already so dry.

The frog pushes out its sac, further and further, until it is like a second frog on the window. Its eyes continue to turn and turn, pointing in different directions like a funhouse toy. It almost looks distressed, like it doesn't know what is happening to it, just another poor, hapless victim. The sac is almost as large as it, throbbing with the rhythmless song.

Just a little pick. Just a little bit of skin.

She reaches up, and her fingers scrape along the edge of her eye, almost nicking the schlera. She finds the dry, raw section, and scrapes off a piece just until it begins to hurt.

Guilt pushes its way from her throat. She hates that she's doing this. She shouldn't be doing this. But it's still there, little hard crusts and crystals along her eye, and a glob of clear jelly at the corner.

The frog's eyes roll terribly, spinning in their sockets. She finds a fat dry piece of skin and—

The sac bursts, opening up the frog like a flower. The eyes spin and fall, rolling down on trails of tissue and nerve. Red blood and yellow pus smear on her window as the frog's skin slips away. She clutches her eye. Blood seeps beneath her fingers, dripping down the back of her hand.

The worst part is the guilt. The guilt of knowing she should stop. The guilt of knowing she can't tell anyone because they'll think she's insane. It's hard to seek support when you have to disclose to your friends and loved ones that you're trying to claw the bacteria from your skin and body. The thing is, it could be *anywhere*. It might live in the little sacs of bacteria in your pores. It might be festering in your bones, building into abscesses that will crack you open. The worst part is that they should know that she's not wrong.

"But they're *supposed* to be there," she says aloud, mimicking the voice of an imaginary debate partner. She leans into the mirror, scrubbing her hands, the skin growing soft like mud preparing to dry and crack all over again. Her eye glares back out from the pore, brown and raw and red. She knows it's not true that the skin is feverish because of the eye, but she can almost imagine the eye like a pustule, like the protruding end of a zit pushing through her skin. This is a big one, this pore is infected. This pore is full and ready for popping. The frog bursts in her mind, releasing the bacteria that were killing it.

Are the frogs supposed to be killed by the bacteria? She should have listened to the radio, because then she'd know if the frogs are dying because of it, or if it is just part of their lifecycle. Maybe they mate, and grow the virus, and die. Maybe this is all natural, like a cleansing, like a purge. Maybe they're supposed to give up the sac and burst it. When she pulls wide the lid, the eye rolls and flicks, finds itself, finds the other in the reflection. It's not meant to be there. It's not supposed to be in there. It's infected. It is an infection.

Just a little bit.

"Like I said, it gets worse when I go out," she says, releasing her hands for just a moment to gesture upward. "It just builds and builds like steam, and when I get home it's worse. If I've been out for hours, or been around a lot of people, it just gets *worse*."

Another clink as her therapist sets down the glass. Drinking again. She feels it building up in her like a coiled spring, like all her blood and guts are rising up into her throat. It all pushes against her tongue, her bony palate, her sinuses. The silence stretches like a frog's wet skin under a shoe, bulging outward.

"You're sure it's not . . . I don't want to make you self-conscious if you're not already, so don't be, but you're very covered up today. More than usual."

Oh, that's useful. Just phrase it like that, that'll help. "No, I'm not *self-conscious*," she says. "I just—I was already talking about how I'm not sure what's the best precaution. That's what's stressing me out. I just don't want to touch anything. And I'm just—I'm just trying to do my best."

Her voice breaks. His is concerned. She wonders what she would see on his face: worry. Pity. Judgment.

"Sure, sure. No, exactly, I don't think that's a concern at all. There's a lot of variation in personal risk tolerance levels, but that's not what I mean."

"Okay . . . ?"

"It's just, usually I can at least see your eyes."

Love In The Reem

It was honestly funny how guys thought Christine's matter-of-factness about big life stuff was so threatening. As if she couldn't be seriously interested in a guy and *also* good at relationships, instead of falling over herself like they did around her. Guys felt the same way about Christine's obsession with true crime—at first kind of cute and shocking, but then they started to wonder if she was planning to kill them. Which wasn't even remotely why she liked true crime. Christine just had a tendency for weird shit to happen around her, and she felt she should be able to spot it. That was all.

Now, Dylan hadn't been either of those two ways. He had already liked true crime before they started talking about it together, and he was *also* a fan of the Wine and Crime Club. They had talked about that podcast the first night they met at Zach's, talked about it for hours in fact. So maybe that was it, Christine thought. Maybe Dylan was a little savvier than the rest. Maybe that was why she was falling for him.

Because despite being a relationship pragmatist, here she was with Dylan, waiting for bread under the fairy lights, and her heart was going like a trapped frog bouncing. It would have been a warm Tennessee night even if it weren't February, and Christine was in a light jacket, yet she was still sweating underneath her plastic gloves and white mesh veil. Across from her, Dylan appeared to be faring no better in his suit jacket, and he kept tugging at the collar with his polyethylene hands. His face was invisible beneath the swaying black veil made of that kind of material they make gym class jerseys out of, but she imagined his cheeks were probably red as the Valentine's hearts scattered across the tablecloth. He was the kind of pale Scandinavian blood that turned a livid hue when he blushed, part of why she thought he was adorable. She resolved to make him blush at least once every day as long as they were together. It was a stupid little promise, but it made her feel warm inside.

So maybe romance wasn't all bullshit.

"What a nice night," Dylan remarked. His throat was clearly a little tight, and Christine thought it cute that he got so nervous around her. He just wanted everything to go right all the time, little ex-honors student perfectionist. "I was so worried it was going to rain and we weren't going to be able to sit outside."

"Of course you did, you nerd," Christine said, because when *she* got nervous, she started to tease him mercilessly. "You also probably wrote *Talk about the weather* on your notecards for when you can't think of anything to say."

"Okay, ow," said Dylan, injured, and she remembered he couldn't see her face to know she was joking, and so she put her hand across the table for his. He laced his plastic fingers through hers, the gripping ridges of the gloves rough and warm against the back of her hand. She hoped that this counted as an apology. "That was a low blow."

"I'm sorry," she laughed. At the table over, a woman wore a very thin white veil with fever-red lipstick smudged off on the inside of it, leaving a bloody smear. Christine imagined her own awkwardness bleeding through just like that, invisible to her but obvious to everyone else, and tried to be fucking normal for once. "I'm an asshole, seriously. Tell me about your day."

The sky was muddy brown, but bone dry. Beneath the patio, the water of the Splitridge Swamp lapped at the supports, and the crooning of the red-frogs sang all around like a Venetian serenade. Someone had scattered the accoutrement of Valentine's Day over the patio and restaurant like pox. When she entered, she had passed through a veil of hanging paper hearts and a pair of sliding glass doors plastered with stickers of cartoon red frogs with Cupid wings. Some people might have found them in poor taste, Christine guessed, but honestly, they were kind of cute. You couldn't be doom and gloom all the time, after all.

At their table, beside the bucket of stinking bleach sanitizer, a bloom of red roses and wax flowers sprayed out from a center piece, their petals and leaves threatened by the candle flame nestled within them. Christine was reminded vaguely of an Advent wreath; there was just something about it that felt religious, like it was promising that something would arrive.

Dylan laughed his big, awkward laugh, and began telling her how Zach, Kev, and he were going out again to look for the mill house. Christine sat up with sudden interest like a dog perking up its ears at a can opener.

One of Christine and Dylan's joint true crime obsessions was, of course, the alleged murder of Jeremy Ries. This was one of the very first things they had talked about—the evidence pointing toward Colonel Langley, who could have set the fire that killed Hieronymus Johnson, the question of whether the mysterious "E. Haskill" had been a victim or accomplice—and since meeting each other, they had only both grown more fascinated with the story. Obsession fed obsession, after all, and Dylan and his crew were already explorers of a stripe. With Christine to bounce things off of, they'd been going out more and more lately, which Christine *loved*.

And Dylan's story today had her on the edge of her seat. He, Zach, Kev had all drove out to the mill house ruins, the site of Johnson's demise right out on the edge of the marsh. Before they'd reached it, though, that idiot Zach got the truck into a patch of mud so deep it nearly took the thing off its axles. When Dylan went down the road to get help, though, he happened across a man named *Sline*.

"Do you know him?" Dylan asked, which Christine told him was a weird question, except that she *did* have a habit of encountering strange people, and she *did* have a habit of adding them to the running list in her mind of people to check up on if a strange murder ever occurred. She'd rehearsed, multiple times, the kind of information she would tell the cops if something truly fucked up ever happened in town. For instance, that harlequin performer who hung out by the Temple but wasn't an employee (she'd *checked*), or that lady with bug-eyes at the Wawa counter who had told her *in detail* how to cook red-frogs, or that guy all in black rags who had followed her home one night, standing just outside the circle of the streetlight. She had actually almost called the cops on him, but he vanished as soon as she picked up the phone.

Vincent Endwell

This Sline, though, she hadn't met. As Dylan relayed, it looked like he lived in this small shack, all rough wood with no windows, and he was sitting out down by the marsh, waxing an ancient rowboat. He was wearing outdated clothes, a style that a workman might wear in the 70s—a patterned red shirt and worn leather boots. When Dylan approached him for help, the man Sline looked up with these *eyes*, pale in an already pale face. They were gray with cataracts, but the man seemed to have no trouble seeing. When Dylan finished explaining, this Sline said nothing at all, but simply got up and walked away along the edge of the water.

Baffled and annoyed, Dylan went back to the others, but as they stood around arguing, they heard the growl of an engine back down the road. Sline had come back with an old rusted truck with a winch, and after some effort got their truck pulled out of the sinkhole.

"Oh cool." Christine had to admit to herself she was a little annoyed that the guy ended up being helpful. "I thought he was going to come out with a gun."

"Well, but then he warned us that we shouldn't be in the marsh," Dylan said, leaning forward. And technically his forearms shouldn't have been touching the table, but it had been sanitized anyway, and what was the risk, and Christine wanted to hear the story. "He just kept saying that it was going to be a bad one. And that those 'Bible-thumpers' in town weren't going to be happy. Which . . . " His shoulders rose to his ears and lowered back down like weakened pneumatics.

Christine told him that the story was fucked up and she loved it, and Dylan said that he thought she would. He seemed way more at ease now that the awkwardness of veils and polyethylene and Valentine's Day formality was fading past. He was so funny like that—such a sincere guy, just wanted to do things the old-fashioned, proper way—but he should know the way to a girl's heart was by telling a bizarro creep story. She insisted that next time he went out to try to find the mill house, he *had* to take her with.

The server arrived with water and to take their order. A second passed where Christine couldn't tell their gender, and the plastic server's veil, cut with tiny holes and printed with pink hearts, sucked up against their mouth like a baby suffocating on a plastic bag. The voice was high, so Christine thought *girl?*, but she wasn't quite sure. There was something not quite right about the server's face in its outline against the plastic, something not a face's shape. And there was something about the set of her brow and eyes, as well, half-visible through the translucent print. It almost seemed like she was glaring at her. Like this waiter hated her with a fire low and deep.

They were saying this year's reem was worse than usual, though Christine thought people were overreacting. A week ago someone had yelled at her in the store for taking her gloves off for a minute because her hands were sweaty, which seemed insanely extreme. It was just all so stressful anyway—people should cut each other more slack. Caroline in particular was the worst about it, hiding in her house all the time and barely talking to anyone. They'd had a blow-up a few weeks ago, too, and now Christine was waiting for an apology that probably wouldn't come.

You could buy veils at every dollar store now, too, but this one she had ordered special so that her mother would stop yelling at her for wearing the disposable ones instead of the ones she'd kept in a box for decades. Her mother believed they made them better the last time the reem came; Christine was honestly not convinced, but didn't want to argue.

"So," Dylan said, with the kind of low pronunciation that meant the start of a new conversation. His shoulders were tight, and he seemed to be knotting his hands underneath the table, plastic whispering against plastic. "Chrissy. Can we talk about . . . us?"

Christine's pulse quickened like someone realizing that the dance has started around them and they need to get in time. Usually she was the one asking these questions—it was rare the guy took point. "Yeah, of course," she said. Her chest actually felt tight, as if her heart inside had grown more lobes like a blooming flower. "So I feel like it's *pretty* clear we're dating at this point."

Dylan chuckled with relief, scratching the back of his neck again with a little more vigor. "I mean, I think so. I like you a lot, and I could really see a future for us. I'd like to take it a step at a time, but I'd like to keep, ah, keep talking about it with you, and such." He gulped like one of the frogs by the water. It seemed like he had approximately half of a rehearsed statement, and had reached the end of it.

"Me, too," she said sincerely, chin on hand, skin touching glove. Should she? Well, whatever. "Do you think we should work through some of those early relationship questions? I know I've been thinking about—we should talk about what we want and where we see things going. Like, are marriage and kids even things you want, long-term?"

Dylan took a sip of water, carefully timed, lifting up his veil just a little at the bottom to slide his glass beneath. The water glass slid out of the veil and he wiped his lips on the back of the polyethylene glove, beneath the black mesh. Now, you were really not supposed to do that, but again, *everything* was sanitized. Admittedly, there were some dead frogs lying on the sidewalk to their right, and the restaurant was pretty close to the water, but, like, what can you do? Not live your life?

His answer was up-front: he did want marriage, and he wasn't sure about having kids—not for a few years, certainly. That was really hopeful, because that's about where Christine was. She dove into it, how she definitely saw herself married and had a few ideas for a wedding, but she had never been that into kids and would have to really think about it. She had a lot she wanted to do with her life and her career, and Dylan seemed really positive about that. He nodded, said that building the tutoring business was important, and he said it in a way that felt honest, not the kind of affect guys put on when they want to support your dreams but are going to turn around later and wonder why you're not in the kitchen.

He surprised her next with a question of his own—what were her dealbreakers? She had to think on that for a minute. There were a few more red-frogs on the pavement by the water, warbling like a choir at gunpoint, some of them scuffling with each other like bulldogs having a fight. A lot more of them were dead than alive, she realized, little red bodies littering the mud like autumn leaves. Many of the shops on the boardwalk were boarded up or else the cracks stuffed with fabric, and the windows of the apartments above were cellophaned in layer upon layer of foggy plastic.

Movement behind the glass of one apartment caught her eye, and she paused mid-sentence to make out the shape. There was a person standing behind the glass, blurred and ghostly and watching, gazing down at the street and the diners and the water. The person moved, and she saw that they were wearing a veil which she had mistaken for a curtain, they were standing so still.

"A dealbreaker. I mean, probably someone who doesn't take the reem seriously," Christine continued, more slowly. Her gaze kept being drawn back to the person, standing motionless behind the glass. She started to wonder: if she missed one person, could she have missed more?

Oh: she had. There were more people in those windows, in off-white veils like hanging drapes, all gazing down to the gentle lapping of the mire. Her skin started to crawl with the realization that they must have been standing there the whole time, or else moved very slowly into place. Maybe they were waiting for a parade? Fireworks? An advent of something?

"Though, not as insane as some people are about it, obviously," Christine said, warily. "I mean, if you're taking super unnecessary risks, that's not good, but like, I don't know, you have to go out for mental health reasons sometimes."

As she spoke, she dipped her hands into the bucket of bleach and sanitized the palms and backs of her gloves. Like a contagious yawn, Dylan did the same, rubbing bleach over his gloves and trying not to nick the edge of his suit jacket. He nodded along, and gave a thick little cough, like he had a frog in his throat—ha, ha—and was trying to hide it.

Christine considered. "I guess that applies to anything. Like, housecleaning. I think like . . . reasonable levels, you know?"

A sudden clatter of footsteps broke through the noise, and Christine spun to look. A black-clad figure emerged from behind the white buildings of the boardwalk and raced down the cobbled road. For a moment, she almost thought she recognized the person, and grabbed Dylan's hand before she was sure.

But it wasn't the man in all the black rags who followed her that one time. This person *was* dressed all in black, though. Their footsteps pounded like sudden drumbeats, and Christine's heart pounded faster, no longer just from the incipient crush.

The person careened up the brick street of the commons, racing urgently like the emergency surgeon's knife. It was not so strange these days to see someone covered from head-to-toe, but there was something costume-like about this person's clothes—the shorn rags, the tight bindings on their legs, the slippers that so neatly danced around the dying bodies of the frogs on the sidewalk.

Then the runner slowed, staring at the restaurant and its outdoor diners through that dark feathery veil. For a moment, they were only about twenty feet away, looking right at Christine and Dylan. Christine's skin crawled, and her throat suddenly seized with sandy dryness. She crunched Dylan's fingers beneath hers, looking for reassurance that she wasn't crazy, that this person really was just *staring* at them.

Then the person croaked loudly, with a voice muffled and hoarse and strung through with incredulity.

"Idiot lovers of plague!"

Heads turned across the patio, swaying in their black and white veils. Christine flinched, sudden shock crawling up her spine as the runner continued, voice tolling and falling against the rippling water.

"Disease-spreaders! Sickness-bearers! The frogs love you! The frogs worship you! You are fuckers of frogs! You are married to bacteria! Your children will be pestilence and vermin!"

Silence hovered like an archway about to fall.

Then the person started racing once more like time was limited, time was running out, dodging around the frogs like a hopping heron and vanishing into the dark. People started to chatter, gossiping and discussing with first confusion, then anger, then laughter. Christine released her grip on Dylan's fingers only long after the figure had left sight. The white-veiled watchers, unnoticed by the other diners, stood still in the windows.

"What the fuck," Dylan said.

Christine laughed uncomfortably, trying to shrug off the feeling coming over her like a chill. "That was so fucking rude. Also, incredible timing," she said. "That's exactly the dealbreaker I mean. If you start, like, *berating* random people, it's totally over."

Dylan laughed roundly. "Great, I'll remember not to do that."

"Wow, really glad we had this talk."

Christine sipped water to clear the blockage from her throat. She felt all tight inside, and it hadn't really lessened since the start of the date. She must have been more nervous than she thought for all this pressure to be inside her ribs and jaw. She actually started to feel the onset of a headache, like her stress and nerves and general sense of romance had all crawled up inside her skull like mice inside the drywall. The sip of water did nothing, just made more obvious how dry and hot her throat was. The faint taste of bleach didn't do much for her either.

"Actually," she said, rasping a little, "this is exactly the kind of weirdo I attract, for whatever reason. So maybe that should be your dealbreaker if you date me. Whatever curse I have is going to rub off on you, and you're going to start getting all sorts of creeps around you as well. Like *Sline*."

Dylan squeezed her hand. "Honestly? That sounds awesome. I would love to encounter crazy weirdos with you any day."

Christine laughed, but also kind of meant it. Her heart fluttered again, seaweed in a warm, shallow current.

"By the way," said Dylan, and reached beside him to a bag he had kept hidden beneath the table. He pulled it up and set it on the table (which he probably shouldn't have done—contact-mediated disease and all that, but whatever), and it was red and glittery and Christine was already excited, despite herself. His voice warbled a little again. He was *so* nervous, and he gulped, a broad and silly sound. "I was going to wait until later, but now actually seems like a really good time. I got you some presents."

The waiter came back, and there was a little flurry as she left their plates before them, but honestly Christine barely noticed. Dylan pulled out a wrapped package and handed it to her. She struggled to open it through the gloves, and so she pulled one off and set it to the side. When she pried open the paper, she gasped with joy.

It was a bullet journal, with a soft cover and an elastic strap around the side, and it was printed with something she recognized immediately—the original typewritten text of Jeremy Ries' last work, *A Pyramid Fit for a King*, which was entered into evidence in Colonel Langley's trial and conviction for Ries' murder. It was the same color as the yellowed paper, the strange and haunting words wrapped all around, and it was exactly the kind of esoteric and macabre and *fun* that she loved.

"You know me *so well*," she said, laughing, flipping through the soft and round-edged pages. Her heart was full to bursting. "Dylan! I swear to god you asshole! You know me so well!"

He laughed, looking at her in a way that (she imagined) was

full of endearing happiness. "I thought you might like it. It seemed like your style. Organized, pretty, murder-related."

"You asshole, it's so good!"

"There's one other thing," he said, and pulled out an envelope. Christine took it. In the corner of her eye, she realized that the waiter never actually left—she had been standing just a little ways away, with what almost looked like a cruel smile on her face beneath the heart-printed plastic like a proper weirdo. Ignoring her, Christine slit open the envelope and pulled out normal printer paper—and then realized what was printed on it.

Two tickets to a live taping of the Wine and Crime Club—happening here, in town, down at the Lenore in just a week. They were recording an episode on *A Pyramid Fit for a King*.

There was a sudden high pitched noise, and she realized it was her, squealing with excitement. Distance and touch be damned—she got up and embraced him, squeezing him to her with all her strength. His face felt misshapen beneath the veil, but she must have been wrong, it was so weird that they had to wear all this fabric all the time.

"How did you know?" she exclaimed. "Was it because I talk about this all the time!? Oh my god, Dylan, this is the *best*, you have no idea how excited I am!"

The singing of the frogs rose into an orchestral crescendo. Ripples lapped in the water like tongues. Someone coughed at a table nearby, wetly. Dimly, something clicked in her head and the thought crossed her mind that the reason the waiter's face looked so misshapen was because of bandages, wrapped around their chin and head over some kind of injury or protrusion. Had the waiter even said a single word? Had she heard her speak?

"I thought you'd like it," Dylan said, and she could hear his cute little smirk, even though his voice was a little thick. "I figured we could go together next week—it should be a really good show."

He really was adorable, and he really was thoughtful. She wanted him in her life, sharing every weird moment, visiting the sites of murders and arson, laughing at the macabre. The heat of the moment rose, and she thought, God, it was so stupid that they couldn't just kiss, they were already eating food, outside, by the edge of the water, and she lifted his veil and hers and pressed her lips to his.

Heat rose in her chest, and her heart expanded again. A lump seemed to grow in her throat and just behind her eyes. His tongue tasted odd, swollen and feverish, and the heat of the crush and the chill of disgust fought in her like scuffling frogs. She couldn't seem to catch her breath. As she pulled back, she noticed a lump in his cheek, like a jawbreaker pressed against his teeth. Dylan was completely flustered, absolutely Valentine-red, and he laughed again.

Then when he spoke, that lump protruded like another tongue beside his, poking out of his mouth. It was an eye. Bulbous and frantic, the yellow iris flicked in the fleshy socket like someone looking for a person in a pushing, shifting crowd.

"I'm glad you like it," he said, sloppily. Another eye roved beneath his cheek, yellow and peering, a curious bystander. Confusion, fear, dull happiness blurred in her. She reached up and touched her own throat with her unclean gloves, and found a lump bulging beneath the skin like a ripening fruit.

The coughing around them grew worse. People doubled over their meals, lungs heaving damply, roundly. Dylan started to cough again as well, and this time it was productive. Eyes, each hanging by a long viscous red string, fell from his mouth like egg sacs, or a bloom of flowers. More and more sagged from his mouth, filling his mouth, becoming his mouth. Christine's head throbbed like it wanted to split, little viscous balls cracking their way from her skull like a shell. They pressed and oozed beneath her dress, between her ribs. Her head throbbed with the eyes behind her eyes, and her vision turned warped, then red, then black.

And for a moment there was nothing.

And then sight reemerged, fractured, flicking many uncontrollable directions all at once. She watched, she stared, she gazed, and she saw him right before her, and all that hope and liking flowed out like a font. Eyes dripped down her face like tears of joy, each telling her with bright and glittering detail that *romance wasn't dead.*

And it was just like having a crush, like the pressure built and built until she couldn't take it, but also, felt just wonderful. Amidst all the torturous confusion, the amorous bafflement, the anxious, agonizing beauty, she wouldn't trade it away for anything.

"I don't just like it. I love it," she said, and her words fell muffled and thick through her mouthful of staring, roving eyes. "I honestly can't wait. You've made me really, really happy."

ISLE OF THE DEAD

HE KEPT DREAMING of Recorsona, the lost island, the Isle of the Dead. It would scarcely let him sleep.

He hadn't lived in the complex long. Mere months, actually. He hadn't planned to move to Olyoke from Nashville, but there had been a job posting at a museum, and he hadn't been able to turn it down. Out of cash. Though it reminded him of the little town he hated, he didn't mind it here that much. No one knew him.

And the complex wasn't such a bad place, either. Older apartments, but converted well. The building was stodgy brick, but there was light, hot water, new renovation. The place had been built for construction workers in the eighties, he was told, and then when the theme park was complete the place emptied and became decrepit, overgrown. But then it had been bought up and restored. Either way, it was a fine place. Comfortable. Convenient.

But the dreams... They came on suddenly, and before he even had a name for them. A name for the place: Recorsona. O Recorsona...

He dreamed of a place of mysteries and wealth, death and wonders. The trees were black cedars, spires toward a dusky sky, and the faces of the people hidden and masked—cheerful, staring mummers. They were actors in a play; they were laid out on the slab. He arrived, each night, on a boat paddled by many people whose heads were wrapped in silk, or bandages, and he paddled among them, with them. Yet he could see the isle approach, and so his eyes must have been undisguised, and yet he sat and labored with this faceless, silk-wrapped crew.

Red rock and sand, and tents and festivals, and the gaping maw of the isle's tomb like a mouth with rusted, vibrant teeth. As the crew disembarked, they unwrapped each other, such that they saw with new eyes. His hands became wound with the silk from other's faces, a grand nightly ritual.

And the isle filled him with vibrant longing, such melancholy that he had never known. He woke up certain he was nearly there, certain he had arrived and walked with those strangers in motley on this rocky shore. He splashed water on his face, and when he caught sight of his face in the mirror he began to weep, knowing that he was locked back away in his own skin.

Because on the isle he was someone else. On Recorsona, the Isle of the Dead (*O Recorsona ! You whom we never reach !*) he walked with a man all in green, a whistle on his lips and cheer in his eyes. The man addressed him as Lady Meliora, and the dreamer, he wore a gown all in ochre. He must have worn some mask on his fine face, for he could feel it, and feel the smooth skin and lips painted in kohl and carmine. The man in green met him in many of the dreams on the shore beneath that gaping tomb, and he would lead him to the festival, glimmering halls draped in ribbons and cloth, frozen at that last night before the sacrifice.

There, they would partake in food and drink, wines all shining pinks and oranges, and food that he had never seen before, and could not name, and could not recall the taste. And those others at the party, they all greeted him like an old friend, and he knew he was loved by them, and he loved them. When he told stories, stars and chains darted between his palms, dancing with vivid life. He felt celestial heat draped over all of them, the sharpness of sparks and the chill of chained gold.

These friends of his, they were conspirators together; there was something grand that was coming. They, too, spoke often of their love for the land and the isle, lively and damned. O Recorsona ! they proclaimed. It had fallen from grace. It had fallen like a ship on empty waters, sailing toward the starless void. O Recorsona ! It had once fallen out of the eyes of God, and now cut off from all, it languished and decayed.

When they walked, the whistling man led him around the shores of the isle, away from the setting sun toward that encroaching, restful night. Along the porticos, struck with sage and heather, the man in green swept an arm out over the sea. To the east, a fell wind blew, hot and dark and gleaming.

And it was there that the dreamer saw the end of the sea, that peril, the void which approached. The sky was indeed as starless as the tomb that sat above them.

O Recorsona , lamented the man all in green. We are not what we once were. We are not what we were once meant to be.

No, agreed the dreamer. We are a ruined people.

Not yet, said the man all in green. Lady Meliora, you are still fine.

We are fine, said the dreamer, because we have chained the stars and brought them here. We are the people of stars, but they will not burn forever.

Of course, said the man all in green.

Why must I leave every dawn? he inquired. Why cannot I remain here? When I return, I feel sick to my core, certain that I will never return. That I cannot ever return. Why cannot I stay here?

And as he spoke this, he felt the tremor of that awful fear, that he would never be Lady Meliora again, with her soft skin and long arms, her beautiful gowns and sweetness of voice. She would be cut off from him forever, and Recorsona (*O Recorsona ! You whom we cherish and mourn !*) would fade like a dream that lingered, poisoned him from inside of his very heart.

You have answered this yourself, said the man in green. The manacled stars can only do so much, and burn for so long before we have expended them. We are not a ruined people, but we are a cursed one. Not for long, however. Not for long. I have designs, you know.

I wish to never leave, he said. I know I cannot have this, but if I cannot have this, you must at least let me look upon that which lies in the tomb. You must at least give me this.

The man all in green sat quietly in that fading, gold-red dusk, and then looked at him with a maleness that was not the sort that came from intention or desire, but a look of a co-conspirator and confidante.

Meliora, he said. I can do this. But I am afraid that if I do, you will be too scared to return.

I must know, he said. I must know.

Tomorrow night, said the man all in green. Tomorrow, and I will show you.

Above them, the tomb gaped like a mouth. Nothing could be

seen in the blackness within, but it was as if it took a sudden breath, and all the candles on the isle danced, and even the colors of the sky itself seemed to shudder, as if suddenly drawn toward it.

When the dreamer awoke in his comfortable, renovated apartment, he threw himself from his bed and scrubbed his face until it was raw. The new lights and fresh wallpaper mocked him with their flatness. Above him hung the image of the tomb, chained stars shedding no light. The wind still seemed to crawl like dead hands over him, and the thought of what he would see in that tomb chilled him like the touch of the void. If he were to look within, he knew, he would not return, could not return, and he didn't know whether he meant never return to the island, or never return to the land of the living.

The terror drove him. He packed bags full of everything he could reach and threw it all into his car. It wasn't long before he was well away from that comfortable old building, far away from the odd little town, driving with a fury. That darkness haunted him, and the fever of chained stars against his smooth, hairless skin.

O Recorsona ! Found with such difficulty, and so easily lost. O Recorsona, Isle of the Damned !

Pyramid

"**The problem with** you is you're too *sweet*," Frank said, lolling out the word like rejected gum. "And I know you're not actually that nice. You should tell them what you really feel and stop letting them walk all over you."

Unspoken was the implication, *You should be more like me.* Damion didn't know if he would like that. Certainly, Frank seemed to spend less time in outward worry and regret, but to call him a happy man would smack of sarcasm. Damion scraped a thumbnail in the grout of the tile wall, pressing the phone to his ear over the rattle of carts and gurneys, and worried pointlessly that they were falling apart.

"Yeah, probably."

"Yes, probably. Say it with me. Yes, probably you should tell Kevin to fuck off and just meet me over here."

Damion couldn't tell if the tension in Frank's voice was anything more than the usual high-tuning and distraction. He often felt that he was like a fine antenna for Frank's moods, able to pick up on the subtlest fluctuations without ever knowing the frequency. Frank would say if he were having an emergency, though.

"I'll be off at seven. Okay if I swing by then? Will you still be there?"

"Yeah, sure," Frank had said, as if already bored with the conversation. Damion knew he wasn't, but he never believed himself with any particular conviction. "I'll meet you. See you then."

OLYOKE

The log farmhouse was swaddled in yarn-dark leaves like an old man draped in a shawl, a wrinkled bark face peering out. Red-frogs peeped like a phone left off the line. Latex powder and the soapy smell of liquid sterilizer somehow still surrounded Damion like a shroud, as it always seemed to for hours after a shift, just one of those things you learn to live with.

The headlights petered out like a wish you give up. Frank melted out of the shadows of the porch light as Damion approached, making him jump. He wished Frank would stop bringing him out here altogether. Damion was happy to take the boxes and furniture Frank gave him wherever they needed to go, back to Frank's house, to goodwill, to the dump, but something about setting foot in Frank's grandfather's place just set him on edge. Like the moment before you push an IV into a vein and you feel the rush of adrenaline as you need to get something right without causing someone hurt.

"What did you want me to see?" Damion asked. One low dim light was burning over the kitchen table, and the windows were open to the dead summer air. "I got Tastee's." He put the bags on the table, the smiling yellow happy faces grinning up like someone holding in a joke.

Frank sucked in air, his hands thrust deep in his pockets and shoulders hunched as if to emphasize his skeleton. Now that Damion was looking at him closer, Frank did seem energized—a fretful, bubbling energy that could still either be disaster or discovery. Words seemed to sit on the tip of his tongue like a grasshopper preparing for a leap.

"Right. Well, I wish you had been here earlier when I was freaking out. Now I'm pretty sure I've just lost it, so maybe we just take dinner and go home."

Damion frowned. Pouty statements from Frank were nothing new, but that didn't make them any more interpretable. "What?"

"Well, the issue is I can't say *what*, and that's what's stressing me out," Frank said, hunching growing more severe. "I could start with the bit where I guess I'm going crazy, but that doesn't really cover it. It would really simplify things, at least."

"Frank." Damion stopped him. Now it was obvious there was something wound up inside Frank like a tangled piano string.

Frank looked up from his raven's posture, his black t-shirt hanging loose on his form. It was like there was a glare in the backs of his eyes, like he wasn't completely looking at Damion at all. "Want to back up?"

Frank's mouth tugged on a self-loathing thread. "Yeah, well, see, if I spit it all out like a joke, then you'll think it's a joke, and we can go home," said Frank. He laughed like sticky sour beer, and then picked up his keys, a pocket knife, and a flashlight from the counter. "I want to go home, you want to go home, we all want to go home."

He headed into the darkened house, and Damion followed like a toy duck on a string, not at all certain what was going on, but with a snarl of dread in his heart.

Frank was nearly done clearing out the house after his grandfather's death a few months prior. It hadn't been quick, nor had it been particularly painless, but somehow the end had still been sudden. After the months and years of hell, the worst bit was that it somehow still came all at once.

Damion had seen him in the ward, though he had recused himself from care. He had tried to convince him, via Frank, to check in sooner, slow the descent, but Greg had been an independent, lonely man, cantankerous until the end. The only glimpse beyond was the note he had written on his last night in shaky handwriting.

The tail end of the note had been brief. "Frank—I know I am making the right choice because every day your grandmother speaks to me and tells me how much she wants me to be with her again. I promised I would join her in our pyramid, and so I go. I love you so much. -Grandpa."

Finding that had been the only time Damion had seen Frank cry. What the old man had meant, Damion didn't know and didn't want to ask.

After the end of that ordeal, there was still all the mess of a life to deal with. Damion had helped a lot with Gregory, because after all he did work in the clean ward—transporting people, keeping track of medications, keeping people company—but something about the sorting through the accumulation of a life did him in. All those years of belongings, odds and ends, notes left to yourself that you'd never follow through on. Damion was surrounded by the failing of bodies, but it was how fast you faded when yours was gone that cut him to the core.

It didn't help that Frank grieved with black humor. He had cleaned out his grandfather's desk by crumpling up everything that wasn't an important legal document and chipperly three-pointing it into the waste bin while Damion had tried to surreptitiously fish them out and ensure they weren't treasures for the family, what little of it remained. As far as he knew, the only ones left were Frank's mother and brother, and neither Gabby nor James were the "taking responsibility" type. But still. Damion felt that being forgotten was a second kind of dying.

Frank flicked a few lights on as they passed through the house, but Damion soon realized why he'd grabbed the penlight. The basement was lit only by a lonely bulb that hung from the ceiling like a moth in a web, and the light tapered away like pattering steps past a tattered sofa, shredded rug pad foam, an ancient lurking furnace.

"We haven't even gotten to work down here, have we?" Damion said with low dread.

"I have," Frank said. "A little." He flicked on the penlight and opened the door to the other half, where Gregory's workshop had been. "It just boggles the mind how the old man had so much *stuff*. Not even a little attempt to think ahead to how he was probably going to kick it soon and get rid of his entire shelf of Kewpie dolls. Found *that* in the other room today, too."

"God, really? Why did he have those?"

"Some of them were probably worth something. Unfortunately, I'm not bringing cursed dolls into my house. Kewpie dolls always look like they're filled with bugs and secretly thrilled about it."

"Hm, no thanks."

Frank laughed like a hinge breaking, a little too sharp.

The flashlight lit up sawdust-covered workbenches, rusted tools hanging on racks. Dust and cobwebs crept in like a bad guest. There was little sign of what Gregory had worked on until they reached the back of the room, where half-finished projects sat about, nothing finished. A curio cabinet was nearly constructed, but missing shelves, glass, and a coat of varnish. Some kind of puzzle box, disassembled, and a chair that all seemed to be carved out of a single piece of dark wood, or else was sanded so finely that you couldn't tell.

In the very back of the room, a grandfather clock stood against the wall. It was wedged in among a dresser and a listing bookcase, its face pointing profoundly to nine in the evening and a broad door set in its stomach. The curls and carvings of the wood were intricate and classic, though vaguely Egyptian. It was a strange mix between Black Forest curls and edelweiss, and hieroglyph depictions of walking people, pitchers, and what looked like stars traced along the lines of unknown constellations.

Frank curled his hands in his pockets, regarding it. Perhaps his fingers were aching again. "You know, when I was a kid, I really thought granddad's house was magic. Like, I would come here and he would do card tricks and I really believed he knew something about the world that no one else did, you know? He was just that kind of guy, that kind of gruff, weird old guy that just seems like if he knew something crazy, he would have kept mum about it. So I'm hoping it's just the stress of everything that's making me think that's true."

His words hung incomprehensibly in the air like a marshlight.

"I can see that . . . " Damion said. "So—"

"I don't know if I should explain or just show you," Frank decided. "Maybe I just show you, and if it's there, great."

Frank studied the door of the clock, and then approached, penlight and knife slotted in his curled left fingers. Damion didn't understand what was happening, and assumed it was at least partially a joke. He half-expected the door of the clock to open with a spray of coiled fuzzy worms like the old peanut brittle gag, or reveal a zany dancing puppet show.

Instead, as the latch clicked and the door opened, Damion saw a light.

At first, he thought there must be some kind of mirror inside that was reflecting the penlight back at him. It was a quiet, dusky light, blue and yellow around the edges like crumbling paper. It filtered from the back of the little cavity, behind the hanging pendulum. Frank took in air like the first part of a curse and stepped back.

Damion crouched and peered in. Even with the penlight pointing at the floor, the evening light remained. It was past dark outside, and he couldn't understand where the little window could be opening to make that light. His mind cycled through possible explanations. The window in the clock's chest seemed to point into the side of a sandy embankment, the soil tinged iron-red. The lip of the sky was barely visible over the top, like a watcher peering over the side of a fence.

A diorama. A convincing set of mirrors. A screen. As Damion crouched before the door, he caught a wisp of air, fresh and hot as an electric shock next to the moldy, rasping air of the cellar. It felt like a discontinuity, like when you remembered a dream as if it were real life and then were told it never happened.

"What am I looking at?" he asked.

Frank started to laugh behind him, and when Damion looked back, there was a grin like a broken door on his face. "Unhinged," one might call it.

"Read the inscription," Frank said.

A growing concern in his chest, Damion turned back around and found a little brass plaque hammered into the interior of the door. He traced the letters with his fingers as he read, the sandy slope and evening sky in the corner of his eye.

"For my Annabel. I would have stopped time for you, but all I could do was preserve it. -G. Z."

It took an hour of investigation before Damion was able to convince himself the clock wasn't a figment or illusion. He looked at it from every angle, shone a light into the impossible aperture, even moved the clock away from the wall and rapped on the back, while Frank sat on the workbench and told Damion every time he tried something that Frank already had. The kicker was when he reached a set of fire tongs in, and retrieved rust-orange dirt from the hill within, and Damion stood with the sand in his fist, soil from an impossible place.

Eventually, Frank suggested they eat dinner.

Under the kitchen light where a brown moth made a nuisance of itself, Frank gripped his chopsticks in one half-clawed hand, hidden effort pressed around the edges of his face. Damion barely tasted his bok choy.

"What should we do with it?" Damion asked.

"Chuck it," Frank said pointedly. "County waste takes large items, maybe we get a return on something."

"No!" Damion said.

"Why not?" Frank's mouth screwed up as he raised his chopsticks to his lips, hand shaking, dropping rice.

"Because it's impossible. And clearly your grandfather made it," Damion said. "For your grandmother, at that. And there has to be a reason why it . . . You're not serious."

Frank shrugged. "No, probably not." His mouth screwed up as he raised his chopsticks to his lips, hand shaking.

The tremor came out worse when he was under pressure, shuddering from the effort it took to defy his cramping muscles and damaged nerves. Frank had been a promising pianist, half-classically trained but who had ditched lessons to form his own style, playing back-up for a little folk band that he loved. Then it had started to pain him—the low, throbbing ache that he had just pushed through, which turned into tendinitis.

He didn't talk much about anything that hurt him except with dry disaffection. It had ultimately been Damion who pressed him. The piano had been the one thing that kept him from sinking fully into fuck-up-dom like the rest of his family. It had been something he could offer the people who raised him, point to and say, *See, I might be the way I am, but you did alright.* The pain had started getting bad at the same time as Gregory's health started waning, and just as his grandfather had wanted to hear the music most, he stopped being able to produce it.

Frank's voice had cracked like a twig. It killed him. Damion had pulled him close, not sure about the right words as always, but at least he could be a presence, someone as sturdy as a wall. That's what he told himself, at any rate.

It had been after this confession that most people would be brought closer. Frank, however, seemed to limp away like a dog with a cut paw. Damion cycled between wondering if he had done something wrong or if that was just how Frank was, closing himself off after any moment of vulnerability. He often wished he could go back and tell himself, just leave it be. Don't ask questions, don't pry. He felt like an otter with a clam, as if by getting Frank to open up, (which had felt like such a true, good, communicative thing to do!), he had broken him somehow.

Damion sat back, green leaves hanging like a limpid from his chopsticks. He wouldn't have been surprised if Frank hadn't been kidding. "Well, okay."

"Probably it was a gift for her that he didn't finish in time," Frank mused. "He never really finished much of anything, as far as I can tell."

"When did she die?"

"Decade ago. He didn't work very fast."

Silence unspooled. Damion's thoughts drifted to that bruised dusk sky and that gasp of hot, dry air. What must be over that hill.

"I have actually been reading some of grandad's stuff," Frank admitted, fishing for more rice. "You know how he took notes on everything by Johnson he could find? He had a book by him that he'd put all his notes in, and obviously I didn't read the whole thing, but there was this one section on 'building your pyramid.' Like, the guy was obsessed with preserving yourself after death and like, keeping your legacy alive. So I guess he was trying to make a pyramid for my grandmother."

Wrapping your mind around it was like trying to get too little paper around too large a box. "But the sand, and the hill—"

"So Johnson treated the world like a puzzlebox," Frank said. "And architecture, built right, could open it up like a key. Or however you open a puzzlebox. That's why all his work has so many weird angles and strange symbols and all that. He was trying to open up little wormholes into the world and find some greater truth, I guess. And I guess he was right." Frank sounded almost irritated by that fact.

He reached into his bag and pulled out a little red leather notebook. The cover was battered but sturdy, and he pushed it across the table to Damion. "Read it?"

Damion pulled it across slowly, as if it were volatile.

"I found it inside the clock," said Frank. "He—never talked to me about any of this, and I wonder if it's because he thought he'd figure it out before he went. Or, I guess, if he figured it out, he'd still be here."

Damion's brow furrowed, Frank's words glancing off like a wrong key. The book felt unnaturally heavy in his hands, as if gravity's string tugged on it more strongly than everything else.

Damion worried. He worried all the time. Few people knew this about him, because at his job he put on airs of calm reassurance (because he had to, because he dealt with people who had it so much worse), but his mind always whirred, rhythmically checking everything that could be wrong. Old habits died hard. He worried whether the medication he gave his patients was right. He worried about his sister and her recklessness. He worried about Frank, and Frank's health, and whether Frank was happy. He worried both that he was a bad boyfriend and that Frank took him for granted. He worried he was too much and too little all at once.

Gregory Zielinski had been a worrier, too. Gruff and reticent in life, Damion hadn't realized the depth of Gregory's fear. Some of what Gregory worried about was the same—whether Gabby would always be the way she was or if she'd ever think about other people, whether Frank would be able to play the piano again, whether James (though he called him his old name) would get through school. There was a bigger worry, though, a fear that pervaded everything he did. One that weighed on his heart every day at the end of his life and gazed forward, past when he stopped being able to affect the world.

He was afraid that nothing would last.

What Damion had gleaned from Gregory's old papers, salvaged from Frank's efforts, was that he clearly had interests he had never talked about, at least not to Damion. At first from Frank's crumpled rejects, Damion had thought Gregory might have been an artist—many of them were covered in stylistic diagrams of things like stars connected in nonsense constellations, cities stacked on top of one another on stuccoed Mediterranean arches, children ringed around a fountain the size of a skyscraper, spilling waves turned yellow by the aging paper.

This notebook was similar; diagrams surrounded by reams and reams of text. It was small, cramped, and partially in German, but much of it seemed to be about the architecture of Hieronymus Johnson, the strange local idol. Gregory had been very into his work, copying over whole passages of *The Red Sun Building* about how architecture was a puzzle box that could pry open the world in new ways, and how one must always be working on their pyramid—the place where they could be preserved. It was the sentiment of an artist, one who wanted their work to last the ages.

It hurt to read. It was the writing of someone who had cared deeply about an artistic immortality, who had never, to all appearances, achieved one.

The drawings were beautiful and meticulous, almost scientific: illustrations of sandstone arches, impossible architectures, plants blooming from statuary heads, all annotated with numbers and measurements and connecting lines. The sketch work culminated after months and months into a design he drew again and again, refining, exploring, perfecting: A grandfather clock, its empty inside spilling out backwards, interior overlapping with interior overlapping with interior, so that the belly of the clock curled out and away like a cornucopia in fractaline reduction into an infinite space.

The distance inside the clock is infinitely long, Gregory annotated, five years hence. *The time the light has to travel is short. Therefore—distance is time, and time is distance. If all places exist in time, so all times can exist in a place.*

Damion flipped through more years, more frantic notes. Gregory's health declining, his handwriting shakier, much like Frank's own early arthritis. Notes about treatment, the occasional reference to Frank coming by. Years of work and development and study. The architect Johnson was referenced again and again, as was the need for preservation. Gregory worried that he wouldn't finish in time.

Then on August 3rd, he wrote, *Finally, it works.*

The handwriting was cramped and small, and cold night air crept in the window and chilled Damion's back. The strangeness of knowing that Gregory had been working on this all the while his health had faded, while Damion had known him, was uncomfortable, like gazing into the past from a different angle.

It works, and I looked, and there is nothing. Johnson must have done the same, or had some other way of knowing what is coming, and it is horrible.

Damion felt something twist up inside him, but he couldn't make himself look away.

The clock opens to the plane of time, Gregory wrote. *The*

Vincent Endwell

mechanism works, and that other dimension exists as Johnson thought. The desert of time is every place, and no place, and every time, and no time at all. According to Johnson's math, the desert expands like a cornucopia, where the space between times is large for times close to the present, but shrinks ever inward the farther you go. The longer you walk, the more time you will have traversed, exponentially. So I did not know if that age would catch you all at once, or if it would only sweep upon you when you were no longer outside time and wear you to nothing like those old feet in the desert. Even walking the length of years might be enough to do me in, as I am now.

I made my preparations before stepping in, but it still did not feel like a real possibility that I might meet my end. I have never really believed it, for all I am so afraid of it. If that's a foolish way to be, then, well.

The desert air was cool, but the sand was warm as if it had been heating underneath the sun of a long day. While there was light like an evening sky, there <u>was</u> no sun I could see in the heavens, and perhaps that is because it has already sunk, or there was never one at all. I first went to check that I was truly in the place I believed myself to be. There were holes in the ground at gridded intervals, some tiny and some larger, and as I peered into them, I realized they were glimpses into time, apertures from the desert into the past and future. The time of my own life was close to the clock, and so I needed only to take a few steps down the slope and gaze into those apertures to see moments of my life.

As I walked, I saw the course of my life in reverse. First I saw my own death: I was in the hospital, and it was nighttime, and I was alone. It was a quiet affair, a slow breath, and then a life to lead in full. I looked back farther, and saw my many lonely years of work, projects unfinished, gaining friends one by one as I went backwards. Annie at the end, also in her green hospital gown, and the worst day of my life was only the size of a pinhole in a camera.

Then there was sickness, then health; all our golden years together, visits to Chattanooga, love-making in the cabin we rented by the lake. Visits from Frank and James, as taciturn teenagers, then as children, and all the fun we had. Arguments with Gabby in the kitchen as Annie rocked Frank. Gabby's wedding, a beautiful and strange day, as we did not love the man *but we loved her, despite how she is. Annie and Gabby and me at the house on Parish Street. Gabby's teenage years, then childhood, then the early terror of having a child, then the pre-birth anticipation. Annie and I on our honeymoon in Nashville, our wedding, our first date. Meeting Annie while I was still in the service. My old childhood friends, my first Communion. I saw the birth of my brother, and then a birth of a brother I didn't know I had, who died while I was only two years old. I saw my own first year of life, and my mother's lonely sorrow. Then I was born, and I was nowhere.*

Annie and I, we lived a whole life together. It was short, and it was hard, and it was wonderful. It was all we got, and we were cheated. Every one of us who lives on this wretched planet is cheated, and we should all be furious every day of our lives for how we are swindled and robbed.

Damion remembered sitting with his mother in the hospital, he and his brother and his father all in a military line on hard plastic chairs. When the thought had sprung up in him that she might not make it, he had had to escape to the little hospital bathroom, his baby-fat teenage face screwed up red in the mirror as he tried to weep silently. He hadn't wanted to upset her. Then another day had passed, then another, then he came home from school and saw his father at the kitchen table, in a chair his father never sat in, and knew that it had happened.

Everything could be lost; everything would always be lost. In the expanse and sweep of time and fortune, everything would be lost. You could cling to pieces, photographs, belongings, but that would only slow the process. Frank had stopped playing piano by degrees; first a few hours less practice, then days. Their apartment had gotten quiet, and Damion had asked, and it had taken him looking Frank in the eye to make him open up and tell him the diagnosis. Frank hadn't wanted it to be real, hadn't wanted to have to explain. Denial ran in the family.

Damion still wasn't sure if Frank hated him for it.

I looked at our life, and I wanted to know. To see, at least, if anything we had made would remain, if anything would be preserved. I only have a little time left, I know I do, but it was not too late to save something, if I could. So I stopped looking backwards, and I looked toward the future. There was that incline in the desert, and I started up it, step by step. I had to rest many times; my hip felt like it was breaking in my side, and I really am getting old now. I don't know what there is of me to preserve. But slowly, I made it up that hill.

As I did, I saw the lip of the hill before me, and a horrible feeling was in my gut. It felt like I was about to lose my lunch, and I couldn't even tell you how I knew there was something bad there, but it was like when you see the look on their faces, and you know. I considered going no further, but I had to know if there was anything that lasted. I had to know if it all meant anything at all.

God, I don't know that I should have.

Over the lip of the hill, a light burned. At first I thought it was the fading light of the sun, but no. It was on the horizon, but it shone with a different light, a red-white brightness that was unlike that waning warmth. And as I saw it, it was as if I flew toward it, until it was all of my vision, and I could see it rising above me. I was suspended in the space between it, in the space between two grounds. It was a world all of its own, something celestial and so vast that it exerted its own gravity, and it fell towards me and I fell toward it.

And I was filled with a dread so incomprehensible that I struggle even now to speak of it. That world was one of ruin and flame and hideous dancing and nauseating laughter, and it broke through the chaining of the stars which had held it back, colliding ever swifter on a course which I had no power to stay. When it collides, it will be with all times at once, with the entirety of our world—not at one point, but with everything it ever was and will ever be.

I will not tell Frank what I saw. I wanted to shout until my lungs fell flat. I wanted to scratch the sight from my eyes.

It will not come this year, nor the next, nor the next. But soon. Soon it is coming, and it is all coming to an end, forever and ever. Nothing will be saved. Nothing we've ever done, nothing we ever cared for, nothing. My entire life, swept away like rubble. What was the point of it all if not even the tiniest sliver of a scratch remains?

I just do not know what else I can do except get as far away from it as possible. The desert is not infinite, but it is vast, vaster than any human could conceive. Perhaps if there is something at the start of it all, it will all mean something. Perhaps there, there will be answers. It is what I have to believe, because to think that there is nothing else, nothing but that terror that is coming . . .

If I walk past this country, past the middle ages, past the Romans, past the Egyptians, past the Sumerians, farther and farther, then it cannot catch me. If I can walk to the lip of time, then at least I will have a thousand thousand thousand years to make my presence known to those people beneath , to build something enduring. With all of time before me, perhaps I can make something that will last as long as anything can.

I do not want to end. Annie, I didn't want you to end. I didn't want it to be so brief.

When Damion looked up, Frank's head was down on the table, exhaustion having crept up on him. His hand curled limply against the wood in perpetual injury. Breath rose and fell and the old house creaked. The hour crawled past ten like a person thirsting in the desert, slowly. In a way, Damion could believe that time could be seen through a pinhole, because sometimes time moved so fast you couldn't see it at all and sometimes you got stuck in a moment, like a room you enter and can't remember what you need.

He closed the journal and took the penlight from the table.

The air in the basement held its breath. The light scattered oblique across the foam and concrete, shadows peering behind objects like spiders lying in wait. Damion picked his way across, rational mind still fighting with itself. He wanted to check that the desert was still there, like he would a dosage. He didn't know what he would do if it were.

He just hated how everything was lost.

When his mother died, he had held onto as many of her belongings as he could—a ring, clothing that still smelled like her, pictures and trinkets. Obsessively, he tried to keep the living room and bathroom the way she'd kept it, imagining her terrified ghost among them as her home slipped further and further from her grasp and she saw her family forget. Bit by bit, though, pieces had to be given away. There was just too much, and slowly her presence in the house dwindled until it was only in these faded mementos, and then barely them.

He knew it was part of grief, and he knew it was part of life, but for all Damion tried to be a rounded and reasonable person, there was part of him deep down that was a little seed of resentment. As long as he could remember, he knew that it wasn't true, that nothing had to be like this. No one born had asked for it, none of it was fair. The lone light bulb hummed pitifully as he stood before the unusual clock, its varnish dark and its carvings arcane. In the woodwork, stars stood on charted paths, and he could believe they marked out a grid of the universe, moments sketched out thousands of thousands of years before they happened, everything in orbit around each other.

The latch on the door clicked open, and dusky light spilled out like milk from the back of the pendulum box. Damion kneeled before it, peering at the rocky sand, rippled by a wind that must not have blown for time infinite in all directions. It was with dark, anxious little nagging roots inside of him that he realized he would gladly look back in time for an eternity, walk among glimpses into moments he remembered and missed and had been too anxious to enjoy. Every stage of his life, he missed the last, and the way it had felt and the people he hadn't said the right things to, and the people who faded into nothing. He wanted so badly to just be able to relive them, to watch them from the outside.

Wasn't that horrible? So many platitudes about living in the moment, about experiencing your life, but weren't they all cheap? Weren't they just a way of assuaging that ache in the soul of humanity, a creature that can do nothing about the raging river of time destroying everything it loves?

Behind him, the stairs to the basement creaked, and Damion turned to see Frank padding over. Frank's t-shirt was rumpled, and his eyes were tired but soft, that too-tight spring inside him unwound. Damion got to his feet, wiping his eyes, as Frank opened his arms.

"I'm sorry," Damion said.

"Why would you be sorry?" Frank said with a low, loving exasperation.

"I was thinking of—"

"Going in?"

"Yeah."

"I figured." Frank's arms tightened around him, balled fingers against his back, and Damion breathed in his smell: Chinese takeout, stinging hair product, their pillowcases in the morning, sweat and dust. His breath caught in his chest that this, too, was transient—this was a smell he would never quite catch again, in a moment that was impossible to keep. "That's kinda why I said chuck it. I thought you might—well, I know this gets to you."

"I'm sorry."

"Stop that."

"Sorry—"

"Damion."

"No, I—I'm sorry for making you worry. You're the one who's going through everything, I'm just here, he wasn't even my grandfather. I'm sorry for—I'm sorry."

"You're fine. I'd rather you just tell me when you're fucked up rather than trying to be all tough or whatever. Then I don't have to guess."

"Are you sure?"

Frank let out a little laughing breath. "Damion, you're too nice. And you're too nice because you're scared of people getting mad at you."

Damion shut his eyes against the dark, and tried to pull himself out of cornucopic layers of self-doubt and interpretation, the one where he was in the present and things were as they seemed, and all he had to do was listen and react. It was like crawling over cold sand toward water. "I mean, I am. Obviously. But it's not because I'm insecure. I'm afraid I'll *hurt* people, and it'll be the last thing they ever hear me say. Everyone goes so fast, you know? Everything happens so fast."

"You're not going to," Frank said. "And I'm not going anywhere."

Which was false, but it wasn't a lie.

Frank released him like a held breath. "Come on," he said, and crouched before the door of the clock.

"You're going in?"

"We are. Just to look. I want to see what he built."

Damion's tongue felt thick. "Okay."

Frank's face tightened with the pain of gripping the sides of the clock, and then he slipped through. The belly of the clock was just barely large enough for Damion, his shoulders and stomach scraping on the wooden sides.

Sand dryly hissed beneath his feet, and the air was open, but still unmoving. Damion had the sense that air pushed out around him like someone stepping in dust, and that they were the only motion in this place for a very long time. A hill rose low to their backs, and fell away before them like a bedsheet, down and down to a flat expanse. Beside them, the clock's entrance had become just a rocky gap in the side of the hill, open to the cellar at the moment they stepped through.

Above, the sky hung blue-lavender and clear as glass, the press and caress of dusk. Perhaps like Gregory had written, they were nearing the end of time, and so this was the final dusk of the place outside time itself. In the slow rhythm of Damion's thoughts, it all clicked into realization with perfect clarity. Places were a time, and time was a place, and everything was all at once and forever preserved, and forever lost. Something could stand for all of time, but time didn't last.

Frank took his arm and pointed with a crooked finger over the desert. "Look."

Down across the rolling expanse of sand and scrub and rock and little holes, each step an exponential loss, there was a long, flat horizon. And on that horizon, so far it was like a tiny model, was a city.

No, not a city. The structures were made of yellow stone and sharp lines gridded out with mathematical precision, stepped triangular monuments shimmering with a day's heat now radiating away in the twilight. There were many of them all together, a necropolis of golden rock, but there were no bustling people in those streets, nothing but a distant empty silence.

There was no way to reach that dead city unless you wanted to die there. Every step, an order of magnitude more, and Damion had a sense that human history would be a blip, then the billion years of the earth, and then a desert of nothing but stars on their grids, turning and sliding forever and ever until there was nothing on either side of the universe.

"He built it," Damion said.

OLYOKE

Frank was quiet, but turned and gazed up the slight hill behind them, the one they just couldn't quite see over. As Damion stared at his face, Frank appeared ageless in the desert light, and all ages at once—youthful and round, lean and middle-aged, old and gaunt and yellowed, his hair receding and white. Frank was thinking about what Gregory had said, about what was to come, and there was a moment where Damion thought that perhaps Frank would want to know. Then his eyes flicked back to Damion's, and Damion immediately knew he'd been wrong, and that neither of them had any interest in knowing what lay in wait. It was better not to see.

For an eternity, in the cooling stillness of the desert, they watched the shimmering, ancient city. Then Frank took Damion's arm and led him back through the hole in the hill, into the remainder of their lives.

Queller

"Yet alas alack, of course, for among other cruel histories we must recount the understanding that there would come a Queller, for when the Transfiguration had not yet settled there would be a sudden Aperture, in which there might be something which dampens the fire and slakes our thirst," soeth proeught the raven thinkers, certain of course of their new truth.

But indeed in a time of dire words and unlikeable warnings, it was the case that any good news that came from the beaks of the raven thinkers was heeded and considered, given the tendency of man to despair.

It was in these times that a new voice rang out among the congregations and considerations; yet another contrarian. It was the speaker of the Whistler, a man all in green, with a smile full of teeth and a song in his heart. He warned the people of the town quickly against the gospel of the Queller, for in his words the fire would cleanse the people of sin and dirt, whereinas the addition of holy water to this mix would create but muck and mud. Necessarily, it transpired that those blind ones in the water took unkindly to this, but the people of the town took unkindly to them.

—From the apocrypha of Hieronymus Johnson, 1962. Uncovered from a cache in the house of Colonel Carson Langley subsequent to his arrest.

THE PURCHASE OF the house had gone smoothly. It just so happened it had been on the market for some time, the price steadily declining until it could be gotten for a steal. The realtor kept describing it as having "good bones," which was a transparent way of saying that it was barely fit for human habitation. It was fortunate, then, that Lyle Knox wasn't looking for a comfortable house in which to settle down, as raising a family had never been a thought it had had and was now a near impossibility.

It had only visited the property once before signing, enough to confirm it was the place it had seen in its dreams.

Lyle Knox had been certain the dreams were a sign that things were falling apart, but even after things ended with Veronica, the dreams only got worse. *The worst had happened*, it thought, with some bafflement. Their relationship had ended, not with a bang or a fizzle but with a normal conversation, as dry as one about taxes or the division of household labor. And it wasn't even clear who had ended it, if it was one or the other or a simultaneous thought, sprung from both sides of a cleft head.

"I've never felt able to get through to you," Veronica had said, scraping a half-sudsed sponge around a half-scrubbed mug. "I thought I could, but I see your eyes come to life and the rest of you is dead. It's like you're buried deep within. Or don't go all the way down."

Lyle, unable to break free of the very thing she was accusing it of, was able to say much of nothing for some minutes. Veronica had sighed, and let the silence pass like a distant train.

But despite the catastrophe coming to pass, the dreams persisted.

The dreams began as they ever did that night, with something inane and innocuous and wrong. Knox found itself eating at a diner, an open-faced egg sandwich sitting on a plate before it. Crinkled bacon and hash browns speckled with pepper and paprika mounded like hills, a blanket over a sleeping giant in the miniature landscape of the plate. Above it all, Lyle Knox loomed like an even larger colossus.

Outside the window of the diner stood the House. There it was: look at it. Revival brick and mid-century modern, old and new alike combined into a crumbling anachronism. Weeds and vines cluttered the sides, clogged like hair overgrown. Half-broken windows watched like scattered black eyes.

Across the table, Julian Potato nervously shredded his napkin, tearing it into piece after piece before discarding it, and selecting another. The snowdrift of napkin grew.

"Why are you doing that?" Jonathan Phenomenon asked, standing beside him and holding a waiter's notebook. His rose cross cufflinks gleamed in the hot morning light.

"I'm glad you're here, Jonathan," Lyle found itself remarking. "I can't eat this."

Jonathan turned his serrated gaze toward Knox, like a jigsaw pivoting through wood. "Why not?"

A strange, hot shame rose in Lyle, crawling up its tongue and jaw. *What if he finds out*, it thought bizarrely, *that I am completely empty inside?* As this thought occurred to it, it became real in the dream. Lyle looked at its hands and could glimpse a vacant darkness just beneath the cuff of its shirt. It realized that if it opened its mouth to answer, then Jonathan Phenomenon and Julian Potato both would be able to see inside its mouth that it was empty all the way through. But it wouldn't be able to eat, either. It couldn't possibly put the food into its mouth.

It pressed its lips together, sweating violently, as the sun through the diner window grew brighter and hotter. Thinking fast, it dug its fork into the fried egg sandwich, spilling the yolk through the valley of potatoes like a lava flow. And there, inside the center of the egg, was a worm, white, writhing maggot-like through the sticky, congealing yellow.

"Ah, I see," said Jonathan Phenomenon, and drummed his fingers on the table's edge in his characteristic way. "That is a concern. Julian?"

Julian Potato looked up from his anxious ruminations. "We don't have a lot of time, Lyle," he said. "The headless giant is stumbling in terror, seeking and crushing. It was called before it was ready, and no one runs to greet it. It is lonely, and scared."

A shuddering rumble pounded somewhere very deep and very far away. Black coffee rippled in the mug, and silverware trembled on the table. Sweat poured down Lyle Knox's back as it heaved itself up and peered outside. The sun was too bright to see clearly, gleaming off the window and glaring in its eyes, but the outline of the House still stood. It was too big for the window, as if it had moved closer, or the ground had fallen away.

Outside, the rumble came again, and the sill shook beneath

Lyle's fingertips. Then it came once more, even closer, and it was so low a rumble that it was barely audible, yet shook the roof around them. The emptiness inside it was trying to grow, to answer the call of that rumble, and Lyle forced it back down like a shameful thing, something that the others couldn't see. The emptiness had always been with it, but it disguised it, hid itself well, and now it was threatening to come out, to expose it as something inhuman and sinful.

"Lyle, are you alright?" asked Julian.

The shaking scattered the breakfast from the table, coffee spilling, china smashing. The worm burrowed into the floor, and the building was hollow, and Lyle was hollow, and it was all hollow in the approach of whatever was coming. The shaking was too much to move, too much to run.

A shadow fell over them all, but when Lyle Knox stared up to see what was above them, it could only see the burning light of the sun.

Heat rose from beneath Lyle Knox's bed, seeping like blood through the floor, the mattress, the sheets. Its back was hot and sticky, its chest soaked with swamp water. It refused to take off the miserable pajamas and see the miserable body beneath, and instead went over to pound on the air conditioning unit, which sat panting uselessly into the air. Eventually, a steadier stream of cold air poured out, and Knox collapsed back into a heavy, crushing slumber. It didn't care for sleep. It resented that it needed it.

John Prime thought the dreams were clairvoyant. Knox hoped that they were not.

Seen from across the street, that House loomed like an expanding shadow. From within the crook of Knox's car door, the building's visage seemed to distort the more directly one looked at it, such that it drew the eye like a marble rolling down a sloping basin. Lyle Knox steadied itself against the hot roof, the mysterious letter shaking in its hand. It was not used to its emotions betraying it. Veronica had said it didn't have real feelings, and yet now she was nowhere in sight and its hands were shaking. If it had a heart, somewhere inside it was oscillating too rapidly like a boiler near to bursting.

As was required of a member of the Society of Pursuivant Nazarenes, Lyle Knox had made a study of Hieronymus Johnson, his writings and his architecture. Johnson's early work put forth the notion of the second layer, the escape from the fate, *that-which-was-coming*. What-was-coming was never named, though the other members of his retinue (Ries in particular) certainly did speculate on its nature. Hieronymus' obsession had been with escape—that like a flood or fire, there would be a region that was harmed and there would be a region to which one could evacuate in advance of the destruction. Hieronymus devoted his life to building this exit to another level before the time came when it would be needed.

Whether or not Hieronymus had succeeded was a question of interpretation. John Prime, of course, regarded him as a fool, and perhaps John was right, as he was the only one of the Nazarenics who had encountered the man personally before his death. There was no second layer, said John Prime, for how could there be? Hieronymus' belief in escape was contingent on a belief in a fire that would come, and there was no fire coming.

Jonathan Phenomenon, by contrast, believed that while Hieronymus might have been mistaken about the terminal nature of what he encountered and crafted in his work, it was true he had tapped into some feature of the world, some as-yet undescribed principle which warped and shaped and accessed an *aspect* of the world, which could be *interpreted* as a second layer, though of course was not in the technical sense. John Prime necessarily found this to also be a step too far. As Jonathan reminded them, however, it was an empirical question, no matter how absurd.

Julian Potato, well, who knew what he believed? Everything and nothing, apparently, gullible but sweet.

And Lyle Knox?

The door seemed to shrink as Lyle Knox approached, but as Knox reached the step of the brick house, the building all collapsed back down like the downstroke of a concertina. A line of ants crawled between the bricks, marching along the dark wood of the windowsill and back into the orange flowering vines. The lock, old wrought iron, took a few tries to open, and when the door swung wide, it was into a room narrow and dim.

OLYOKE

Another thing Veronica had said was that Lyle was meticulous to the point of being cold. Knox didn't believe this to be true, but it did believe that it could be slow to react. It stepped through each of the rooms in turn, listening to the groan of the wood beneath its feet, taking in the smell of dust, age, and thick varnish. It ran its wide, white fingers along the edge of a kitchen table, and took stock of the pink-tiled bathroom, a faint calcic line along the rim of the sink. Throughout the entire house hung a stillness like drapes drawn shut, but with shadows playing beneath their hem. In direct contradiction, its hands trembled.

The style was mid-century, oppressive and heavy. Dark wood, yellowed linoleum, and wallpaper peeling down like sloughing skin gave it a gravity like a lead weight distorting a sheet. This had been intended as a hall for that archaic Society, but the signs of this were mostly present in the empty room in the front of the house, a dais at the front, and in the kitchen wedged well in the back. There was a parlor, and stairs that yawned up cavernously into darkness, and that sigil of the eye.

A line of stacked chairs still sat in the gaping meeting room, gathering dust. Lyle Knox lowered itself to one of the shorter piles, hands spread wide on black-clad legs. Hair crawled up its hands, the band of a watch exposing itself, and it considered this with distance, the same way it looked at molding tapestries across the room. Maybe where things had fallen apart was that Veronica thought it was cold, when really it just took a long time for anything to reach Lyle where it was. Perhaps this was also why John Prime considered it an asset when investigating anything touched by Hieronymus Johnson. It was only now, after having surveyed the house, that Knox felt that dread truly penetrate, like the difference between knowing the intruder is in your home and seeing their face in the gap of your bedroom door. Lyle took the letter from its torn envelope and unfolded it clumsily, and its rustle scattered through the meeting room like spilled ball bearings.

"Dear Mister Knox," it read,

You and I are not acquainted, but I noticed recently that the address of 605 Ridge Road had been purchased with your name listed as the new deed holder. I trust that by your mere desire to

Vincent Endwell

own the property you are familiar with its history and nature, but let me please offer myself as a resource, as I have spent the past several years researching the Society Hall and have come to an understanding which may be of interest or use.

Likewise, I hope it goes without saying that you are in danger, bodily and spiritually, and have been from the moment you became linked to this unusual building. If this is somehow new knowledge to you, it is even more imperative that you contact me swiftly and without delay.

155 Gremire Place, Wentworth Building, Beaumont University Campus. My office is on the 2nd floor, Rm. 22.

It was signed *E.S.*, and the letterhead read *E.S. Hammond, Ph.D., Department of Contemporary Archaeology.* Beneath the name was a phone number, which Lyle Knox had not yet called. The nature of the house had not been new knowledge.

As it looked up from the letter, Knox's eyes fixed on a flutter of plaster dust, a few snow-like flakes drifting from the ceiling. It followed their descent in reverse to where a crack crawled across the ceiling like a silverfish. The crack extended back, past the empty brass lighting, along to the corner of the wall.

There, a thick patch of plaster rounded out the corner from ceiling to floor, cutting the angle of the room. As Lyle Knox stared at it, the plaster seemed to widen, as if it obscured a gap much larger than what it initially seemed to conceal. There was an opening behind the plaster in the wall, and that implied that there was another space behind it. Knox rose from its seat, letter folded back into its pocket, and circled the wall into the next room. The wall was thick, and in the little hallway beside the meeting room, there was a patch of plaster on the wall from the cornice to the sideboard.

Lyle Knox directed its attention up.

Along the thick-varnished stairs, there was another opening right along where the wall met the wood, also filled in with plaster. Lyle followed it up, through a dark landing toward the space above the meeting hall. The region above the meeting hall contained dark rooms with thin windows, a dormitory for the members of that since disbanded order, and it was there that the house ended.

Except (and this was such an exception), except for a doorway filled with plaster in the middle of the house, one that led to nothing but an empty wall on the other side. It was a door that went nowhere and could go nowhere, for it was plastered shut and there was no space for it to extend anywhere except into an empty bedroom. Yet Knox stopped before it, in that dimly lit hall, and that dread rose like water in its throat.

There was something behind that doorway.

Lyle Knox pressed against the wall, yet could not take its eyes from that plastered-shut doorway. Like a blow against a bell, the knowledge that there was a *space* beyond it, an incalculable vastness, struck it and reverberated. *The House was not empty. The House was vast.* It felt the floor weaken beneath its feet like a jumper on an unstable ledge, and the sense of standing on a precipice before a rushing void became an intense hum rising through its legs and back. A warning, a reflex, an urge.

And somewhere, deep within the House or deep within its own mind, it felt the pounding, the shaking of heavy footfalls. One after another after another, they shook the ground and the walls and the inside of its own body. The shaking of its hands before its face made sense now—it wasn't mere nervousness, but rather it shook in response to the *thing*, the *thing that was coming*, and *it was coming, it was coming, it was coming.*

The droning of summer insects could have blotted the sun with its noise. The university buildings stood empty save for a heavy pall of dust and heat thick like velvet drapes. Lyle glimpsed a janitor at the end of a hall as it entered, but when it walked that direction, the woman slipped down another hall and was gone when Lyle reached the junction.

The door to Rm. 22 stood ajar at the end of the corridor, sunlight dripping through. Papers and books spilled beyond. Knox contrasted it with the meticulous order of John Prime, each book labeled and chained to the shelf, and thought it might actually prefer this chaos.

It knocked. "Come in," came the call.

Perhaps it had been biased by John Prime's own predilections and presuppositions. The office was a labyrinth, and Dr. Hammond—E.S., as they introduced themself—sat like a spider in the center, knowledge arrayed incomprehensibly around them.

E.S. was of an age close to Knox's own, crow's feet around their eyes. They were Black, and wore their hair in thinly twisted, meticulous locs tied behind their head in a maroon band. Their clothing was a stylish patchwork, a shirt made of warm yellows and oranges and a pair of golden frames like a piece of precise and delicate astronomical equipment. And they greeted Knox like an old colleague, which in a manner it was, albeit through proxy. The disagreement between John Prime and Hammond had only ever been academic, and while John Prime let his curmudgeonly outlook color all aspects of his life, Hammond inquired as to John's health, his well-being, and that of the Society. If there was a petty rivalry between the two, it was easy to see who had won.

"You contacted me about the house," Lyle Knox said, once the conversation opened.

Hammond folded their hands on a closed but humming laptop computer. "I did. I couldn't exactly let you stumble about without a warning, needed or not. What do you wish to know about it?"

"What," said Lyle Knox, "exactly, *do* you know about it?"

Hammond paused, then stood and shut the door to their office. Papers rustled like feathers in a nest as they did. "I am a scholar of outsider religions and eschatology. I have studied a number of end-times cults, most particularly Los Parientes, a since-extinct Floridian Spaniard cult. But of course, the followers and friends of Hieronymus Johnson have been a subject of personal interest. Of his architecture, I have had the most consistent, reliable access to the Society Hall over the past fifteen years. I know quite a lot about it, its history, its location. Simply ask."

Lyle Knox was not quick to react. It considered this repository and regarded all the routes it could take, historical and philosophical. But one question burned most obvious in its mind.

"Why," said Lyle Knox, "have I been dreaming of it?"

Hammond studied its face, a curator interpreting symbolism. "There are a few ways I could answer that question," they said. "Why have you been *dreaming* of it. Why have *you* been dreaming of it. And why have you been dreaming of *it*."

Lyle Knox said nothing further.

"Do you know why Johnson built the Society Hall?" asked Hammond.

Knox had assumed, but didn't know.

"In his later days, he very rarely built anything without a secondary purpose. It was his second-to-last attempt to reach the second layer. His last was—of course- 'Spirition. Which also—of course—failed." Hammond laced their brown fingers before them, contemplatively. "At least according to Johnson's estimation. His goal was to build a Jacob's Ladder to a place of safety, but the Society Hall certainly didn't take him there."

"But there is something still wrong with it," said Knox. Agitation built up inside it like water in an indent in the boards, but didn't flow over.

"There is something unusual about it," Hammond said, with an air of gentle correction. "And certainly something dangerous."

Knox remembered the shaking which had come from somewhere far but rapidly approaching, both above and below and *outside*, on a plane that it couldn't access but which was close, close, closer. "It feels as though it is either calling me, or pursuing me. Why is there a door upstairs that is plastered shut?"

"There are in fact a total of five doorways that are plastered shut in that house," Hammond recited. "As well as fourteen gaps and three holes that resemble ventilation ducts. Most of this was done in 2003, before the last occupant moved out."

Finally, the emotion staggered out like a recluse in the sun. "*Why?*"

Hammond tilted their head, and a clever, perceptive look came over them. "Because the occupant kept getting lost in their own home."

That little revelation sat on its shoulder, singing sweet nothings. To Lyle, it all started to become clear, like grime cleaned away from a windowpane. In their kitchen, against the counter, Veronica asking "Does this feel good? How about this?" and Lyle unable to answer, insisting it wasn't a problem, just let it kiss her. Lying beside her in those quiet middle years, content but wondering what it had missed, what it was missing, what it lacked. Its body had stretched vast and pale beneath it, caverns and landscapes, and it walked beneath in the corridors of its veins, inside its hands, inside the cavity of its chest. There was nothing, or maybe it could see nothing—or maybe it had gotten lost somewhere, like someone in a hall without a light.

Hammond continued: "Every time they went to get a glass of water, or walk to the kitchen, or God forbid leave, they might find themself wandering alone for hours through hallways they'd never seen, rooms they'd never entered. At first it was an irritation, but it soon became hazardous. Hours would pass, they would grow hungry, and thirsty, and tired."

"I see."

Hammond sat back in their chair. "I always did appreciate John and his friends. They always took everything in stride. True scholars don't balk at evidence. Unlike some of my colleagues, I'm afraid. They don't have much time for my work." They fluttered a hand. "But as it is in the academy."

Lyle felt another sentence welling up inside it, and rather than dismiss it, it waited for it to emerge of its own accord. Dr. Hammond seemed entirely willing to wait, and consider. Lyle Knox found itself, despite its own internal confusion, rather liking the professor, and their quick, intelligent patience.

"Can you help me?"

"Depends on what you want, Mr. Knox."

The revelation yipped shrilly, sounding in its ears like a catastrophe, a calamity, a wrong key forced into the mechanism. Lyle found the words emerging. "I'm not a—"

"Ah. Of course you're not. I'm sorry," said Hammond, and the grinding inaccuracy terminated with apology.

There was still a disconnection between the pair of them, but Knox felt an odd relation. They were a different kind of person, weren't they, and Knox felt strangely comforted by the pivot in their voice. They rose, walked to the window, gazed down into the yard between the academic buildings. A fine spray of black hairs climbed their cheek like feathers, and perhaps here was the source of the gap—unlike Knox, Hammond was human.

"I suppose it all comes down to whether you want to know why you are *dreaming* of the House, why *you* are dreaming of the House, or why you are dreaming of *the House*. And also," and here Hammond looked down out of the window, and raised a hand as if making a sign at some unseen person on the grass below, "whether you can do me a small favor."

The first of the dreams had been ripe and furtive, a plum stolen and given without warning. Lyle Knox had been standing in a garden, walls of yellow stucco around it. The trees were laden heavy with fruit of all colors, blues and pinks and violets and orange-golds. The sky was warm, but there was no sun, no clouds, only a sweet light brownish-blue from horizon to horizon, and it was looking for something, and it was hungry, but it couldn't move.

And there at the end of the garden stood the House. Tall and brick, heavy and silent, it waited. Knox tried to move toward it, tried to approach, but it could not. Then it came to be lying down, looking up at that clear, ripe sky.

Its body, large and worm-like in life, now lay in the dirt and the grass. It turned its gaze to its black-clad arms, which creaked open like double doors. Inside were stairways, twisting and combining and becoming twining, nonsensical pathways. Little figures all in stripes and pointed hats climbed these stairs and hallways through its limbs and torso in nonsensical circuits. Up and down, up and down, up and down they go, through portico and over arch.

"Lyle, hurry up," called Veronica from the door of the House. "You need to see this. I want you to see this."

I can't, Vera, I'm made of stairs, Lyle tried to reply, but when it opened its mouth, more stairs emerged, step by step down its throat.

Still the empty House waited, and waited, and somewhere deep inside Lyle Knox there was a shaking, a pounding. *Thud-thud-thud-thud,* and something approached ever swifter up all those many stairs.

Frogs and insects sang in the reeds of the sun-drenched wetland. Hammond led the way along the edge of the marsh, picking out dry ground from amid dirt that sloughed and slid toward the water. Lyle Knox followed with grace. The body, its body, knew where to keep its weight to prevent mud from staining its beetle-black dress shoes, and dirt from the hem of its suit.

"Though Hieronymus was prolific, he tended to avoid the usual sort of eschatology that would give rise to fanaticism," Hammond remarked as they walked along the rough path toward the home of Hammond's friend. "He was not big into prediction, merely description. Some have interpreted his writings as predictions about the end days regardless, but that didn't seem to be his purpose in putting them down. For example: "Missive" reads closer to a work of fiction, but has been interpreted by some scholars as prophecy. I think they're wrong, obviously." The monologue stalled.

"It sounded like you were setting up for an exception," said Knox.

"Oh, right. Well, in a manner," said Hammond, and laughed. "Clearly I get a little sidetracked." Hammond made their way intentionally over a muddy patch, dirt sucking toward the water. "But yes; there is an exception. While Hieronymus wasn't taken with prophecy, others have had no such reservations. Indeed, after the split with Haskill and prior to their death, there was another group that created some writings related to, but expanding on, the ideas Hieronymus had put forth."

"Did this group have a name?"

"No," remarked Hammond. "It does not."

There was another little slope, and then an open space along a dirt track.

"Should I inquire about their prophecy now?" Knox asked.

"That would be helpful, yes," said Hammond, and now there was space for the two of them to walk side-by-side along the track. Out in the marsh there was a sound like a trill and a *pop-pop-pop*, insectoid and confusing.

"What was their prophecy?"

"They had a number, but where they diverged substantially was in their description of the end times," said Hammond. "What they believed was that there were a number of routes *that-which-was-coming* could take. In one, there would be a thing called *Queller*, and it would come bearing a font of holy water, which would serve to quench the rising fire."

"It seems like you're bringing this up for a reason." Knox looked over, and Hammond had a little smile on their lips, beneath lenses turned a brownish-black in the sun. "What is this *thing*?"

"Great question," said Hammond. "It's been interpreted

multiple ways. Most often, it's considered an event. But some have interpreted it to be a person, or a structure. It's compelling, certainly, that there might be something to help dampen the fire when it comes. I'll admit to being taken with the notion."

"I take it," said Knox, "that you believe that something is coming."

Ahead in the marsh, a small wooden shack emerged from the low, mossy trees. Windowless and pinched, it had an overhang above the door that sheltered chopped firewood, a rocking chair, a broom. Water rose close behind it, brown and silty, and an aging rowboat was half pulled up on blocks away from the marsh. It was a relief to be out of the sun beneath the eaves, and Hammond knocked and they waited, water lapping like a distant conversation.

When the door finally creaked open, the gap in the door was pitch black. It took Knox a moment to catch sight of a pale face and a gray eye, webbed with cataracts.

"And who've you brought?" asked a voice, damp like a twisted cloth.

"This is Lyle Knox, from the Society of Pursuivant Nazarenes, and new owner of the Society Hall," said Hammond, as those gray eyes considered Lyle Knox. "And Sline, I believe you owe me our bet."

The man named Sline was white and quite pale, hair the color of aged paper, and he wore an orange shirt tucked into high muddy overalls. The three of them sat at a table outside in the beating sun as Sline counted out three fives and five ones from a crumpled bundle and handed them to Hammond.

"There's something else you owe me, also," said Hammond, even as they retrieved a gift of boxed tea and three books from within their satchel and pushed them across.

"Yeah, yeah, yeah," grumbled Sline, his voice thick with a perpetual cough. "No, I'll do it. I'm not so proud that I won't own up when I've been shown. These the originals?" He lifted the top book and turned it over. The lettering glinted gold and unreadable.

"They sure are."

"Thanks. Marchie will love to see these back." And he turned to Lyle, who had given its pleasure to be introduced and little else, and said, "So how are you liking it?"

"The house?"

"Right."

Lyle Knox paused, and in that pause Sline laughed, a clotted sound.

"I'm pulling your leg, I know, I know. Usually I'm the one who comes by, tells whatever unfortunate has bought the place that they should scram, but doc beat me to it. Haven't been many for a while. So what's the play, doc?"

Hammond looked to Knox, and Knox glanced back. Knox said, "You said you had a guide through the House."

"Yes."

"I would like it."

Hammond nodded. "I want to be clear, you may not like where it leads."

It recalled how its chest had unfolded to a cavern within, and that little striped revelation wandered up and down among the archways and porticos, singing its rapturous song. *To no longer be lost*, it sang.

"I can't take another night of these dreams," said Lyle Knox. "I'll go wherever it takes me."

Sline chortled, "You don't think it can be worse, is that it?"

Lyle Knox said, "Well, I don't know."

Sline grinned a toothy grin.

Hammond got to their feet. "Well, thank you, Sline."

"No problem. I'll let the others know."

"I hope they will not be too disappointed. We all hope that such things wouldn't happen in our time."

And Sline released a laugh like water boiling up through mud. "That's the difference between you and us, doc," he coughed, and stood from the table as well. "You think that one day you'll die and you'd be able to miss what's coming. You're like Johnson, you think the past is a place you can escape to and be safe in. As if."

"Hm," Hammond said.

As they turned to leave, Sline headed down to the water, where he heaved the boat over onto its belly. The last they heard was the rippling part of the water, and the quiet splash of oars as Sline headed out into the marsh, delivering Hammond's message.

OLYOKE

The House groaned perilously on the marshy earth.

Hammond affixed the folded paper collar around Knox's neck with both precision and a scholarly clumsiness, the sort of knowledge that is unused to being put into use. As they fiddled with an important crease, there was much muttering and requesting more pieces of Scotch tape. When they were finally done and Knox stood, it resembled nothing so much as a lamp turned upside down, scratching at its Adam's apple and first itch of stubble. Hammond stood with hands on hips, regarding it with a certain pride, as they explained how they had crafted this guide from their studies of the house and the diagrams of Hieronymus that had been recovered from the mill. It had been a decade of work, they said. "But preparation is never wasted."

On the paper ruff, lines and diagrams interlinked and parted as the contraption turned and folded. After some instruction, Knox soon became proficient in twisting and aligning its many layers like a fan, until the semblance of a route among a twining blueprint emerged like high ground in swamp water.

"This Queller, if I find it," Knox said. "Do you truly believe it will stop what is coming?"

Hammond shrugged, bird-like. "I believe it may help."

Lyle Knox nodded. There was a profound absurdity to this map affixed about its neck, but it couldn't fault it. It was strangely freeing to finally be unable to see its body, to look down and be unable to even check that its shoes were tied. Only the tips of its white fingers could be seen beyond that wide, tea-colored lip. "Very well. John Prime may have questions for you, of course."

Hammond laughed. "He'd better! I worked hard on this."

"Where will you go?" Lyle Knox asked.

"Exactly," said Hammond. "Exactly."

Hammond asked if all was set, and Lyle, flashlight in hand, had to agree. As the scholar left the House (and was that the sound of them speaking to someone? No, it couldn't be), however, the sense of incongruity only encroached, until Lyle Knox could no longer see the door that Hammond had just exited. It stood in the meeting hall; that gap in the corner straining to widen. It checked its cufflinks, both to be sure they were there and to be sure that its arms had not split open, revealing their shameful contents.

"Alright, Knox," said Lyle, and its voice rustled with the paper close about it. "This is it, I guess. I hope Veronica's happy." That hope wasn't a spiteful one, but a genuine one. It did hope that she was happy.

Upstairs, the plaster doorway stood like pale, unmarred skin. Lyle Knox ran unseen fingers down it, and the sensation sent shivers of ice up its spine. Then, without letting itself think, it pulled back its fist and plunged it forward.

It broke through the drywall, the impact shuddering up through its bones. It pulled free its fist and struck again and again, until the hole was as wide as its head and gaped open into the black. With its foot, it broke the hole until it could fit its body through, and plaster dust spilled and settled like strange, choking pollen.

Behind the plaster, a dark and narrow hall extended impossibly into the house. Just to convince itself of the illogical nature, Lyle checked that on the other side of the wall was nothing, just a flat surface through which, apparently, the hallway extended. The dark wood floor was covered in dust, and the walls were plain wallpaper like the rest of the house.

Lyle stepped into the darkness, and somewhere, something shuddered.

It clicked the flashlight on, and before it, the paper ruff lit up with instructions and designs. Lyle Knox proceeded slowly, dust rising from each footfall, until it reached the first intersection. Five hallways split off of a small room, a coffee table positioned in the center. Lyle consulted the paper ruff, rotating it until its designs aligned with the room's geometry. A red mark led it further into the House. It continued.

After this period of its life was over, Lyle and Veronica would be friends again. It could believe that. "I think you'd be happier with someone else," Veronica had said, and Lyle had balked internally, because it didn't feel unhappy. It was happy, but Veronica hadn't seemed to believe it. And how could it explain that it had always felt like this? There was nothing deeper there, no second layer, no unhappiness, no pain. Just room after room, hall after hall. Tapestries hung dust-covered on the walls; picture frames obscured with dust dotted the stairwell.

"I don't think you're happy, Lyle," Veronica had said.

"It sounds to me," Lyle had said, "like you're saying you're unhappy."

"I'm not unhappy," Veronica had said, then considered, her hands paused under the running sink water. "But I'm not happy, either."

"You're right," Lyle had said, taking another dish to be dried. "It is for the best."

It encountered a blank wall at the top of the stairs. Hard wood blocked the way, and Knox paused, light filtering up through the ruff around its neck like a bulb through a lampshade. It switched and rotated the map, but Hammond's calculations were certain: this was meant to be the way forward. Hands searched around the corners of the passageway, hunting for a hidden latch or an unseen handle, and came up empty.

It wasn't as if it hadn't tried to be a good man. Knox stood on the stair, clenching and unclenching its fists in a way that felt alien and distant, like pulling a mechanism to open a distant door. It had tried to do everything right. It hadn't been a very good son, but it had been a good husband. It stayed clean-shaven; it dressed well, in blacks and browns and that permissible cold corporate blue. It had taken her hand in public and put her coat on her when leaving a restaurant, or a play. It had been stalwart, slow to anger, quick to help. Why hadn't that been enough? When people looked at Lyle Knox, they saw the balding head, the doughy squareness, the body hair, the thick-fingered hands. They saw a man. So why was it, Lyle thought, that Lyle itself wasn't as easily fooled?

It walked back down the stairs and stood in the hall, doors and corridors branching out and curving away, and something in its mind was singing a song. The song was simple, wordless, and it curled up through the empty space within its pressed black suit and emerged somewhere around the base of its neck. It was a twining melody with a distant, insistent beat.

It had tried to be a man, because really, what else was it supposed to be? What else *could* it be, in this body? It was a relief that it couldn't see itself below it and all its incorrectness. When it was a child, it had had a recurring daydream that it was just a head, and it would take the head off of its body and let it float free in the air. It would drift like a balloon over the ground, twisting and looking and seeing and never interacting.

Vincent Endwell

Lyle Knox thought of this again, and thought of impossibility. What if what you wanted to be couldn't be done? It was impossible to be anything but a man, and it was more impossible to be what it wanted (What did it want?) But here it stood, in an impossible house with an impossible guide (What did it want?)

It had never truly examined what it wanted to be, because it knew it was impossible. It had always felt such safety in structures, but a body was male or female. A body couldn't be architecture.

Something shuddered far below.

Lyle Knox stood still as the floor shook, picture frames rattling against the walls. It steadied itself against the plaster, and could feel, somewhere distantly, a constant, pounding beat. No, not a beat. Footfalls.

Something was coming.

It was arriving.

Panic crept up in Lyle Knox's mouth, and what a strange feeling it was able to feel, now that it couldn't see its body. It moved the rustling paper guide frantically, searching for its error. The guide still pointed up the stair, but the top of the stair was blocked by an empty wood wall. Knox climbed the steps again and beat on it with its fists, first in frustration, then with more insistence. The wood was thin, and nailed incompletely. Knox wedged its fingers beneath the boards and pried, drove the heel of its shoe into the wall and smashed through. A hole widened near the base of the wall, small at first, then wider. There was a light, yellow like the sun, stretching from an unseen aperture.

The shaking grew closer. Plaster shuddered from the ceiling, and the floor reverberated beneath Knox's feet. It got down on its hands and knees, peering through the gap. Its flashlight rolled away step by step (*thud, thud, thud*) as it squinted against the light, trying to see what else could be removed to let it through. There was wall on the other side, but if it squirmed, if it twisted itself, it seemed as if it could fit through the gap, and then come through.

Footfalls pounded through the floor, *thud-thud-thud-thud*. In a sudden burst of fear, Lyle pushed itself through the hole, battering Hammond's paper guide into uselessness as it twisted its shoulders to fit into the gap. There was more wall on the other side, but a space smaller than a closet extended up toward the light. Knox shoved itself through, and it still couldn't see its body beneath it, couldn't see the hands that scrabbled on either side, couldn't see the insulation of fat, the heavy foundation of torso, the buttresses of arms and legs. It writhed upward, and the body was but a weight dragging it down.

Then its head pushed through the hole, and its shoulders caught. Hot yellow sun beat down in a black-and-blue sky, and dry and dusty grass surrounded it. Its head protruded, hugely, in a field before it where all things were laid out in miniature. Knolls and valleys, tiny blades of grass, distant trees were a model landscape invented before it. A faint wind crested through the field, and above, violet stars burned in a gridded sky, constellations linked as if by golden chains. But despite the size, the dirt beneath it was real, the grass was real, the light of the sun was real.

Where was it? It wriggled, but it couldn't emerge further. It was stuck—just a head in the dirt, looking up at the gaping sun. Reverberations pounded through the earth (*thud-thud-thud-thud*) and a shadow fell over Lyle Knox. A colossus loomed, blotting out the sun.

As the hands of the headless giant took it by the side of its head, Lyle Knox thought, *oh*. The hands wrenched its head back and forth, like one working wire until it snapped. *Oh*. It had felt as if its body had not belonged to it, because its body did not belong to it. The hands whipped back and forth, and the world blurred into a jumble of light and stars and swaying grasses. *Oh*. It had only been a head, and now its body was here to claim it.

Its neck snapped like breaking wood, and as it was lifted, it felt the body beneath it, the creaking boards, the straining beams and nails. Rooms and halls extended out like digits on a hand, and through each window beamed another vision—a town in flames, a town sinking into the earth, villagers running and fleeing, villagers burying themselves in the thick and viscous mud as fire scorched through the sky. The shadow of an unseen colossus fell across the scenes, something massive approaching closer, and closer.

And for the first time, Lyle Knox staggered up on its feet and stood above the little town, a giant among men. And it was finally home.

The Celebration

"Why aren't you dancing? Today is a joyous day!"
—"Elemental Concerns" by Jeremy Ries, as performed by the
Worthy Crafts Theater Company, 1961.

"**Do you ever** have dreams you're somebody else?"

The question caught her off-guard. Maggie looked up from the breakfast dishes and the morning sun blinded her. Her first thought, however absurd, was, *How does he know?*

Because of course he didn't know. She couldn't expect him to know. But the question felt as if he had intuited something about her, gotten a glimpse behind the curtain. Perhaps he had figured out that the reason why she was distracted and exhausted, working herself to death again, was because she *had* in fact been dreaming of being someone else. Every night, she had.

In Maggie Warner's dreams, she was a fat man in a green twill suit.

The man wore an old-fashioned jacket. It was a proud thing, thick-threaded and rough on the fingers like a rug. Dull brass buttons blistered up the front, and he paired it with a moss-green felt hat, a turkey feather stuck in the brim like a joke between him and himself. He had a mustache, thin and bristly, and when Maggie dreamed of him she could feel the stubble on his neck and cheeks, prickling like a wasp's legs. In the dream, she never reached up and touched it like she would if her face suddenly sprouted hair. His jaw was blunt and his eyes were too close together, so that sometimes, when she caught his reflection, he almost looked like a Cyclops, a Polyphemian descendant.

She remembered every detail she glimpsed of his appearance—perhaps because it was so strange to be in a man's body, so obviously mismatched from her thick hairless wrists with their fat bangles, and her sagging face and dyed red hair. She found herself going over every aspect, committing them to memory like a loose thread you keep pulling.

And she didn't understand why it didn't feel worse than it did.

She called him the Whistler, and she had dreamed of him since the last day of teaching, so much so that she had started to feel like him even when she was awake. Always, the Whistler was boisterous, persuasive, fun-loving, even a little cruel. He acted always with his grand purpose in mind—much like herself, she supposed. In her dreams, he journeyed through a city of white sandstone, searching for an item which had been lost to him many years since. He swept an arm and opened a slurry of doors in the sky, each of which led to a field of bloody sheep, an empty, crumbling pyramid, the backside of someone's mirror. And he had been convincing people to join him as servants, aides, or compatriots in a mission Maggie could never remember upon waking. His designs were always needful, and far more important than anything she had ever done in her life.

And real. He was so real.

So that was how Maggie Warner had come to another belief. That was how she knew that the people she met in dreams were the only ones that were real. The waking world was a stage filled with actors, and it was the people the Whistler met behind the scenes that were putting on the show.

She wondered if she had told Bill about him in some quiet moment, one where she loosened her tongue on the intricacies of her insides. She couldn't see his eyes through the hot knife of the morning sun, and so she couldn't tell what he had meant by the question. She wondered if it was an accusation, an admonishment for not being fully present.

"Sometimes," Maggie said, as the diner noises faded out like the background of a radio play. "Do you?"

"Nah," Bill said. He spooned sugar, glittering crystalline slopes falling into rippling black waves. "You know I don't really remember my dreams."

Maggie was certain that she had just been speaking to this woman who had come up to her in the bustling backstage. The woman was short, white, hair cut in a blond bob like a sugar cookie 50's mother, and a mound of costume fabric was bundled in her arms with annoying grace, like she didn't deserve to hold such a thing. She seemed like one of Maggie's least favorite parents, guardian of one of the bratty kids in her classes who would blow off work and ride along on their mother's excessive intervention.

"Maggie, Maggie, are these for the tailor or for the adulterer?"

Maggie stopped the sewing machine again, with reluctance trying to figure out by color and type why she should know what role the fabric was for, when there was an entire pile of sewing still to be done before the end of the day.

But of course she was running the show; it was her show, after all, her creation and responsibility. *The Winsome Daughter* was the name, a composition that celebrated the best part of the town, from the building of 'Spirition, to the legendary time people had gotten together to tow a car out of the marsh, to the construction of the theme park and all other little stories from recent memory. It followed two characters who walked through time and commented on all of these scenes from the past, and Maggie would be lying if she said she hadn't been inspired a little by Ries and his proclivity to narration. She taught English, after all, and as he was a local playwright, she felt she had a duty to honor his works.

And of course no one had batted an eye when she had started organizing it, and no one was surprised that it would be held as the centerpiece of the town festival. She hadn't even raised her hand, just got to work planning, and everyone had fallen into step behind her. Was it too much work for one person? Was she, as ever, bad at delegating? Sure. But everyone knew that was Maggie Warner's way. The end product would be good; it always was.

"Tailor," said Maggie, confident she had just spoken to this woman about different costumes, about the ones for the villagers (the ones who whispered and gossiped while they did the wash, a colorful background crew). Why had this woman stopped working on those? But that must have been someone else—Maggie wished she could remember her name. "Those need to get done today, the costumes for the adulterers can wait. Olivia isn't around to rehearse until Thursday. You need a hand?"

The sense of unreality crept up more intensely, the curtain fluttering before the stage play. The woman who was identical to the other woman swept away with her fabric, and Maggie had to wonder if that had just been the same actor playing a different part. If she were putting on this production, she would have changed the costume design, made something obviously different to fool the audience from far away. This reuse was confusing.

"How does she do it? She just keeps going." From the backstage, Maggie overheard some of the other women remark out in the seats, as the crew bustled to prepare the set as the day grew nearer. "I swear to God I don't know how she keeps up with it all. She must not sleep."

"Ha. No, I don't think she does," the other replied.

How Maggie did it was with a planner of to-dos, sheets of people to contact and organize, and most importantly, the empty void of the summer months when school was out and she needed something else to keep occupied. The churn of her brain required something to gnaw on, to masticate, to stop it from turning its jaws inward. If she was exhausted, that meant she was doing it right.

At the end of the day, crew workers started heading home, one by one, and Maggie wished everyone a cheerful adieu. The last, the blond bob woman (what was her name? What the hell was it?) came up and said, "Are you heading out soon? It's nearly nine."

"I'm just going to finish this up and then lock up," said Maggie, gesturing to the last line of stitching on the villager's dress. "You head on home."

"If you're sure," said the woman skeptically, and Maggie felt the low prickle of indignation. "We don't want you to work yourself to death."

Maggie felt the crease of irritation at the implication that there was a "*we*". And who was this busybody, who acted like she knew her so well? Linda, or Naomi, or Barbara—the name didn't matter, because she was just different bit characters played by the same third-rate actor. Inconsequential to the piece.

Maggie laughed, that good-natured laugh she was liked for, the one that people said really *saw* you. "Don't worry about me. I'll head home in just a few."

As the gossip left, Maggie returned to the stack of costumes beside her, finishing up the final stitches on one and beginning to sew together the disparate pieces of another. Lies, lies. The hours stretched out quiet and thin beneath her, the work engaging enough to keep her thoughts at bay. Usually she would work herself to exhaustion, return home, and from that be able to pitch herself into slumber like a diver into black water: the higher the height, the lower the depth. But tonight, she miscalculated.

In the warm backstage of the auditorium, the rhythmic clack-clack of the sewing machine beneath her fingers, Maggie felt the world shudder and start around her. She had grown too tired too quickly, and knew she wasn't going to be able to make it home. *Might as well keep at it*, she thought, threading the machine once more, and then realized that she hadn't threaded the machine, only imagined it. She tried to thread the machine again, but no, it kept not going through, not because she had missed but because her hands hadn't moved. The thread entered the loop a third time, but no it hadn't—and then the Whistler got up from her chair, rubbing his wide-fingered hands together in bubbling excitement.

It was time for an announcement.

The spotlight clacked on, and sudden tittering rose in the seats, the anticipation of an audience before the show. The Whistler adjusted his cuffs, smoothed out the front of his jacket, and black hair crept up the back of his hands, wrong but also correct, an accurate depiction of something Maggie couldn't see. Glee filled him, the pleasure of finally getting started, of being back at it, of a project now underway.

Then he exited the backstage, emerged into the burning knife of the limelight, and raised his palms for applause. The people in the seats, small though they were in number, understood to clap vigorously and without delay.

" 'He is to be resurrected, my little thief! And it is an honor, to be the one brought back from outside the fire and the blood and the glory. This –' " he intoned, and from center stage he swept a hand across the black of the auditorium, and then across the feet of the stage, and it was certain he was not gesturing to the dream, but to what had come before, the place from which they had all come. " 'All this is temporary. A fabrication. A trembling leaf on an autumn branch. You know this.' "

The Whistler paused and let the sonorous echo of his recitation hang like motes of dust. The theater held its breath as a grin grew on his near-Cyclopean face.

"You all know this," he said, and now he spoke directly to the audience, and faces gleamed into clarity against the dark. They were familiar, and had an earthy corporeality, a *truth* to them. These were people he knew, and knew well. "As I read this play here, you will recognize the words, because you—yes, each and every one of you—is chosen. At some point in the past, perhaps by fate or by fortune or even by merit, you were given a piece of the picture, and you were left sleeping and waiting."

The Whistler spoke with a showman's pronunciation but with sincere annunciation. True caring and delight flowed from his words as he recognized them, named them, called them forth. "But now I am here to tell you that it is time for you to play your part. We are going to put on a show, and it will be a grand performance—grander than any that has been produced. I will need all of you for it. You all are essential. You will all have a role, and when we are through, there will be dancing and rejoicing. You are part of something very, very special."

He hopped off the stage, walked along the first row, and pointed to the people in the seats. Ten, or twenty, and when Maggie thought on it later she recognized them, each a familiar face within the town. One caught his notice for unknown reasons, a familiar young boy with a girlish build, his hair still too long and his arms folded in discomfort across too large a chest. Perhaps it was his expression, an angry face suddenly loosened and open.

"I will come to each of you in turn, when it is time," the Whistler said. "You will know it is me by the phrase, *Why aren't you dancing*? This will prevent any imposter from confusing you in our mission. And you will answer me with the phrase you hear in your heart."

At the last, he turned to them all, and the faces were confused, and hesitant, and excited, and full of interest. "I look forward to working with you all."

And the plan, the glorious plan, the Whistler saw it in full before him. The ceiling opened like a blossom, and those gleaming stars hung above, chained by golden bonds in the burnished violet sky. Beyond, that Planet hung, heavy as a lead weight and bearing down with infinite speed.

OLYOKE

Though the plan was a great burden, the Whistler carried it with ease and with joy and with a spring in his step, because his purpose was grand and his designs were only just underway. Each step climbed upward like a twisting, impossible stair, and he itched to undertake his ascent—for his compatriots, for himself, for that glorious end that awaited, arriving, ever precipitously closer. Oh, and if his enemies didn't find him before it was through, what an end it would be.

As she woke at the sewing bench, sweating and sticky in the beaten lights of the backstage, Maggie scrambled to cling to that purpose. Her body felt base and clay, a blisteringly cruel reality. What had he seen, arcing above in the heavens? What was the plan and the purpose? She needed it, that sense of ambition and clarity, and the details seemed to trickle like sand through her fingers, fading with every second she was awake. But she knew one thing, and that was that she needed to find them.

His accomplices—the real people—were waiting for their orders.

It wasn't that Maggie Warner didn't tire. It was that fatigue never felt like a particularly salient detail. Being a slave to one's needs seemed such a sad thing, she told herself, but that wasn't what drove her to always be moving and doing. No; it was that deep within her, coiled outside the light, was a certainty she didn't *deserve* to rest.

But there was no need to contemplate that, because her schedule was full. In the morning she was meeting with the acrobats for the procession, and then the town clerk to ensure the permit was in order, and then the stage builders for the center of town who would raise the scaffold and dais where the show would be performed, and the team that was making decorations for all the telephone poles, and that carried her through past lunch but she wasn't really prone to hunger, but maybe she could grab a coffee on the way to rehearsal, black with two sugars.

Bill had been the only one to ever confront her. Perhaps because he had been the only one who knew the extent of her habits. Most people in her circuit regarded her hard work with dim approbation, but it had been Bill who would stand around until she agreed to go to bed, encouraged her to take meals and rest and sit down for a while, Maggie, please, you're going to run yourself into an early grave.

She remembered with a sudden flare of anger, like a simmering ember catching a breath, how sure he had been he'd been helping. How *sure* he'd been that he hadn't been making it worse. It was the height of his arrogance that he thought she did this for no reason, and it was even more infuriating that he assumed she wished to *stop*. Had he thought her tasks weren't important, weren't worth the energy expended? Did he consider the energy expended wasn't the *point*?

He didn't realize how much worse it could have been. This, this was better than that churn left unabated. Now that she could plummet into sleep and dream, there was finally a chance of her getting to be someone else.

Now there was the constant pull and fascination, looking at every face she saw for familiarity among the sea of nothing-people. It was good that Bill could no longer hold her back, because it was more important that she found them than anything had ever been.

Was he even real, she wondered? Or had Bill been just another actor?

In the dim lights of the auditorium, as the soliloquy dragged onstage, Maggie found herself nodding. One head snap, then another, and for a moment she was drifting and free. Hailey Temple's country twang started as the play moved through the history of the town, and Maggie drifted, the actors all around her like motes of dust in the air.

One face stood out clearly among them, impermeable and whole. He fixed on it, and they saw each other in that space.

Linda Neuman (or was it Barbara?) shook her awake before the act was over. The music rang in her ears like a phone call she couldn't take, and her body felt heavy, enormous in all the parts she associated with being a woman. She felt stuffed-in, her chest filled-out heavy sacs, her hips bulky as phone books, skin soft and hairless like a baby's chubby wrist. Her eyes were sunken in her head, barely able to see from within the pits of a ghoulish other woman's body. For the first moment, Maggie couldn't move. She was dough, she was clay, she was unbaked.

Then she shrugged off Linda, whose makeup-caked face had acquired a line of insincere concern. Along the way, she ignored others who needed to consult about the lighting cues, diction, the design for the program—flies needling her in her path. She caught the boy as he tried to leave, stepping out of the high school into the sweltering sun.

"James," she called, and he jolted, even as he tried to pull his hood up and evade her. Maggie was faster on her feet than she looked, though, and grabbed his arm as he tried to flee. "James. *Why aren't you dancing?*"

The boy turned back, eyes brown and wide, and she could see plainly that if she had not known him in dreams, she would have mistaken him for a girl. She felt a strange distaste, not unlike when she caught one of her students doing something for which she had been punished long ago. It was a kinship, but one tainted with the sense that they shouldn't get away with what you had long since written off as *not-allowed*.

His words were restrained like a dog on a leash, as if he were testing whether he could even say anything else. But when James spoke, it rang out clear and forceful: *"Today is a joyous day,"* he said. *"It's the day when the sun arrives."*

"He asked you, didn't he?" said Maggie. "You know him."

"Who . . . ?" James said, but it was clear he knew. "Ms. Warner? What's going on?"

"The man in green," said Maggie, and James' eyes flicked around for an explanation of how she had seen into his dreams and couldn't find one, and that was how Maggie knew she was right.

"No one calls me that name," said James.

"They do now, my boy," Maggie said, and she felt the Whistler's presence as she clapped him on the shoulder (a gesture so unlike her), and smiled. It was his smile, and it felt like a light bulb turning on behind her teeth. "These thespians don't realize that you're a different tier of being. The characters in a play don't know they're portrayed by actors, and they certainly don't care about the crew. You will join me. We have work to do."

"Ms. Warner, I don't understand," said James, but he did, and the Whistler had no need for protest. Maggie held up a wagging finger, and he quieted like a sudden wave of nausea.

"He'll be in touch," Maggie said, though her mouth wanted to say *I'll be in touch*. She went back inside, the dark like a kidnapper's blindfold after the bright of the afternoon sun, and wondered if she should feel ashamed. The strange things she'd said, running after the kid. Should she be self-conscious that her dreams had leaked out, like chocolate running out of the mouth of a greedy child?

But she wasn't. That thought occurred to her, and passed like a momentary cloud. None of this here was real, so why care? And there was much real work to be done.

As the festival approached, so too did the other preparations begin in earnest. The Whistler's plans became clearer and lingered longer in the waking world, and Maggie caught herself turning them over even as she ordered the programs and finished the sewing and directed the performance. Every waking moment, she longed to be back in dream, where items and tasks of strange non-meaning had to be performed. The Arcaneum had to be visited, she knew in her heart. The Old Coptic had to be retrieved. And for all this, they first needed the key, and so this was where the Whistler first took James, to test his mettle.

"There will be another celebration," the Whistler told the boy James on their first night. The dream opened with them crossing a river that poured, black and silty, through a tossing solid sea. The Whistler had no difficulty walking on the churning water, while James lagged behind, incredulous at the gaping ocean beneath their feet, surprised to be suddenly dreaming and awake. "It will be quite a marvelous day, my boy, quite a welcome indeed. But to put it on, we need certain things. Things that I, alas, cannot retrieve myself."

"Why not?" demanded James, indignant, as if he thought this was mere overbooking. "How?"

But the Whistler could be kindly. He looked back and smiled. "Old laws and such, you know how it is," he remarked. "Some rules even I can't break. Despite how I'd love to."

In the days following, Maggie had found more of his servants that he had spoken to in the dream of the auditorium. There had been Ursula, the tattooed novelist who wrote at a café and had jumped when Maggie had sat down across from her and ordered a coffee. Amelia, the strained college student who had tried to hide in the library but whom Maggie had found by the buzz of her phone. Sergio, a tired janitor who had been more willing than the rest and had begged to be given tasks, held her hand and demanded it. All were off on their own business, but the Whistler had taken a liking to James. Of the co-conspirators, he was the least deferential. The Whistler respected that, saw something in the boy. Someone quick to learn.

"Or do you just not want to?" James demanded. The sea flattened into land, a sheet of icy obsidian which turned into Tennessee forests, the mountains rising up before them. Frogs sang in some distant marsh or wetland, unceasing. A cabin appeared along the track, a rough bark overhang shading a rocking chair and a shovel. The Whistler stopped and turned to James.

"I very much wish I could," said the Whistler. "When I was younger ... perhaps. But this first item will be easy. Just walk in, snatch. Simple."

It was another testament to James that when the order was given, when push came to shove, he didn't hesitate. When he emerged, he held in his grasp a heavy brass skeleton key, leather knotted at the end. The man inside, James said, had never noticed, but had seemed to become insensate as James' hands wrapped around it. James hid his consternation well, and handed over the key readily. The Whistler knew that for him, James would do better, and worse.

"What do we need this for?" asked James.

"To open the Arcaneum," said the Whistler, "of course."

"And why do we need to do that?"

James had the best questions. The boy's mind was sharp and contrarian, and he had long since burned through the obvious asks of "How is this real? What do you mean? How can you see my dreams? So, are you Mrs. Warner or not?", some of which the Whistler answered.

And a later night, James asked, "So what is the point of the celebration?"

Vincent Endwell

Now the pair journeyed to a crumbling sandstone tower—James quickly like a jumping spider, the Whistler with a slow and methodical pace. The stars teemed overhead like an infestation, and fine golden chains wrapped around them like glittering bangles marking the inadvertent edges of the universe. The roof of the tower opened to the stars above, and there was a scientific reason for this, which the Whistler knew but which faded in agonizing decay from Maggie Warner's mind when she awoke.

The tower opened easily at the turn of the brass skeleton key. Inside was a library, ancient and disordered. Books had fallen from shelves and tables as if in a quake, and now littered the floor and walls. In some places they stood open, half-arranged, as if the last inhabitant had been in the midst of fervent scholarship, abandoned in a rush. The Whistler instructed James to look through each of the texts, for a book he would recognize when he saw. The Whistler, however, stood with his arms crossed in the center of the room, well away from any of the texts. He knew that for him to touch any of them would be a bad idea indeed.

"James, James," said the Whistler, as James sorted through the sea of tomes. "You're such a serious boy. You need to know the *purpose* of a celebration? It's not enough to have fun for fun's sake?"

"No, it's not," said James, bluntly. "I'm a killjoy. What are we celebrating?"

The Whistler chuckled and gazed out over the desert beyond the broken tower. "A birthday," he replied with good humor. "James, do you know the old tradition for births?"

James shook his head.

The Whistler drew on that well of knowledge he had; the one that fell away in the daytime and left Maggie feeling stupider and thick. "It used to be, in this town, in the olden days, we would celebrate a birth by hosting a huge party. There would be flags and garlands and food and trumpets, and we would finish it all off by tying down a bull and cutting its throat."

James flinched, as if a hairy black fly had landed on him, but continued looking through the books as if he had not been shaken at all.

The Whistler continued, callously. "The father would then take the skull and drink the blood from it to welcome in the new life.

And of course, the bull would then be butchered and served," he said. He spoke like a honeyed rubber ball. "Originally it was raw. This was in the days before anyone cared about food-borne illnesses. Welcomed them, even."

James grimaced at him as if expecting to see the blood in his teeth.

"There's no way that's true," James said. "That's some more crazy dream shit."

"It is. I was there when we did it."

James shook his head. "You're like, forty. There's no way."

The Whistler worried so little about whether people would keep up or agree. It was freeing, to not even consider what they were thinking. "Try that one," the Whistler said, pointing to a heavy tome with a red-and-gold cover. James picked it up and opened it across his arms. Curled letters unlike any language on earth squirmed nematode paths across the page, and James glanced down, and then could not look up. His neck jerked and twitched as he tried to, but it was as if iron rods gripped his skull by the sockets, locking his eyes to the page.

Indifferently, the Whistler continued speaking, even as veins stood out in his assistant's neck. "It *is* true," said the Whistler, clasping James' shoulder. "This is why we're having a celebration. It's because something is being reborn."

Around the pair, the letters of the other opened books changed to those of that same alphabet. James' mouth moved as he tried to pronounce words which he could not possibly know how to speak. When the Whistler spoke again, his voice was kind. He felt a sudden fatherly fondness for the boy, his anger and all.

"I know you know something is happening. You wouldn't be helping me if you didn't," the Whistler said. "Now, I don't mean to sound dire," and he laughed, "but nothing unreal will last. In fact, very little is going to last. Because the other world is coming."

James twitched like a fish on a hook as he tried to look at the Whistler and couldn't.

The Whistler's voice grew softer, like fading dusk. "Really, we were a people terrified of dying," the Whistler said. "If only I could describe to you the greatness of our civilization. We built structures that reached the moons of our worlds and dug far into the earth. Our cities covered our planets in buildings tall and yellow as moonsand. We had reached the height of our power, and we were so scared that we would be forgotten. So we did something foolish.

"We killed ourselves."

James' breathing was labored, frightened. The Whistler walked around him, observing the Old Coptic that wriggled like worms beneath a microscope lens.

"We killed ourselves, and from our entombed skulls we chained the stars in their glory. In this way, we made ourselves the shapers. We placed the universe on tracks of our making, but not our design. Though we created the gift of prophecy, we could not control what happened or change our fate.

"This was how we called the Planet.

"We saw it in our skies as first a light, then straining against the chains of our making. I do not know if we changed its orbit as we set the skies in artificial motion, or if it came of its own will to undo the crime we had committed. I have tried to find out, but I have never been able to travel there except in nightmares. The chains across our sky prevented it from reaching us, but we now live a half-life, one of waking nightmares and unfinished lives. In time we will die a second death, and the void will claim our fallen world. Or we can embrace the Transfiguration which comes. We can speak the words that will open the Tomb, and celebrate the rebirth of the world, and be transformed."

There were no more questions left in James' mouth, only sharp pants. The Whistler took pity on the boy.

"Many have tried for so long to preserve what they can, and they think of themselves like Pharaohs building pyramids to protect their earthly bodies. Others think they can quell the fire that's coming." He shook his head sadly. "But you and I know that won't help. Lazarus can't come put a drop on your tongue."

The stars opened above them through the open roof, their gridded expanse spiraling out, their promises thinner and more revealing. The Whistler began to sweat in the heat, droplets beading on his brow, and he knew in his heart that they had very little time before his adversaries came, now that the communication between the worlds had been opened. *Time to go.* He used James' hand to close the book, and as he did James wrenched his eyes away, blinking rapidly. Alphabetical designs shifted and squirmed behind his eyes, now contained within his skull. He scowled as if he could feel them, tilting his head like a dog with water in its ear.

"But why?" he gasped. "There has to be some way to stop it. There has to be something else we can do."

"There are forces arrayed against us that think they can," said the Whistler. "But Jamie, I gotta be upfront, it just won't work. It is already far, far, far too late."

The world felt like cotton when Maggie awoke, pressed in too close. She was a sandbag and mud on the edge of the marsh, and the question of who or what the Whistler feared scratched around in her head.

Later, she encountered James at rehearsal, where he was painting the sets for the performance. In every section he worked on, twists and curls of paint stood out and squirmed like maggots crawling beneath skin. A shiver seemed to pass through every body at once, as the words of the old language whispered at the cracked stone of the Tomb.

He met Maggie's eyes, paint dripping red from his brush. "Are you happy?"

She said kindly, "Great work, James. Keep it up."

The first sign that things were falling apart came right after the sign they were coming together. The festival performance was a week out, and the actors had learned their lines nearly by heart, and the costumes had been made with a glimmering thread drawn from the depths of a dreaming ocean, and the sets brought the scene to life with that uncanny alphabet crawling beneath every panel. The Whistler's servants waited for their orders. And of course in the flat waking world, the programs were printed, the streamers were on order, the performance of the acrobats was flawless. Everything was almost done.

There wasn't enough to do.

Maggie couldn't take it. To be undone by her own efficiency was a sort of irony that she wasn't capable of dealing with. Worst was that in every quiet moment, she could feel the horror creep back in. Perhaps she became micromanaging, taking over tasks that she rightly didn't need to. It was her right, in a way—it was her play. And maybe she changed the script a few too many times, but it needed to be just right. It was good, but it could be *better*. *She* could always be better, and this performance was an extension of this need.

But there wasn't enough to keep her up, enough tasks to push her to that precipice of exhaustion from which she could plunge into dreams. She tried to stay awake, drank coffee, but it wasn't the same.

And then. The accident.

It was a minor fall. And really, she was fine. It was during rehearsal, as she was climbing the steps of the stage to coach the actor playing one of the travelers. She insisted that she just slipped, that her foot hit the stair wrong, but she knew not everyone believed her. She had stopped speaking before she started to fall, and those on the stage must have seen her eyes flutter shut before the descent. All she remembered was lying in the orchestra pit, gazing up at the beams of the spotlight like the intricate bonds of the universe, and weeping.

What scared her, though, was what she saw before she fell. All the actors on the stage, all the unreal people in the false waking world had looked at her, and it was as if something else, malicious and watching, were looking out from within their eyes. What really frightened her was the sense of recognition. As if not only did they know who she was, but she knew who they were, and she knew what they wanted.

The injury was ultimately minor, just a sprain, but because of the risk of concussion, she was instructed to rest. *Rest.* A sick word. No one had ever gotten better by resting (she told herself, she believed this to be a fundamental truth), but then Bill had picked her up from the ER, and he had looked so disappointed. So very . . . Bill. Linda must have told him she was there, and he would have remembered the last time he had been with her in the hospital. How she had put herself there.

And she hadn't been able to dream. Everything was so close, her associates waiting on his orders, and she couldn't get to them. She tossed and turned, but nothing put her under.

"You have been sleeping more, right?" said Bill. The menu was spread out before them in a thick laminated coat, the print fine.

Maggie felt like a deflated balloon, defeated and useless and spiteful like she had when she'd moved out her belongings to a new apartment, fresh and empty.

The split had been mutual, the culmination of years of chafing and squabbles. It had been completely unseen from the outside; for a time, they had been Maggie and Bill, the town power couple. They were on the school board, they put on events at the fire station, they organized the voting drive, they chaired the council for the arts. They had run this town, and no one had known the fights behind the scenes, how much Maggie did on her own. How late she burned the candle working after Bill turned in alone.

In a manner, she had done it for him. Because if that churn was left unabated, it led her to contemplate those other, more permanent, solutions.

"More than what?" Maggie asked, a sort of petulance creeping out. She hated feeling under supervision.

Bill sighed, grimaced. "More than usual. Enough."

"Those are two different questions."

"Maggie, you can't keep doing this."

I can and I will, said some fury within her. From her lips, she said, "Linda's a bit of a snitch, isn't she."

"She cares about you."

She's not real. Maggie sipped her coffee, her ringed fingers clacking against the china. Why did she wear all of these? Was it because the jewelry distracted from the skin beneath? A carapace made of turquoise and silver? "That doesn't make her right. Or not a snitch."

"It's not just Linda."

"Who else?"

"That's not the point, Mags."

"No? I'd like to know who's talking about me."

Bill took a long look at her, and Maggie focused on his hands, broad and flat-nailed, with a nagging envy. If she looked into his eyes, she'd see those blue irises and that perceptive concern that she loathed. Their final conversation, quiet and resigned, played again in her ears—"I don't think I can be with you right now," they had both said, but Maggie had put the emphasis on *I* and Bill had put it on *you*. And she hadn't been mad then, but a slow and cruel anger crept up within her now. How dared he put her under scrutiny, when she had never even seen him in her dreams? She looked up at him and searched for the tells. He was an actor, wasn't he? He never really had cared, and he didn't now—he was just playing the part.

Perhaps it was time she learned for sure.

It was as Maggie hobbled to her car with the uncomfortable crutch wedged in her armpit that she caught sight of a familiar face. James Zielinski hesitated at the end of the block, lagging behind a woman who must have been his mother. He turned to go, but Maggie raised a hand and called out. "Hey! How have the sets been coming?"

She made small talk with his mother, a woman with a pinched face and an incessant demeanor. "A great student, doing a great job with the sets. A talented artist, you know!" The whole time, James' eyes flicked to Maggie's and then away, as if there were something he were holding back. When the short conversation was through and his mother began to head away down the block, he ran back for a final word. "I saw you. Last night. In my dreams. But you didn't know the phrase."

Maggie froze. "You mean you saw the man in green."

"*No*," said James, his voice pitched low in latent fear. "I saw *you*."

She found Sergio first, or rather heard of his passing. In dreams, the Whistler had stationed him to guard the Arcaneum against assault, and so his body was the warning shot fired. He had been found in his janitor's closet in the school, lying with his back over the yellow mop bucket, his face in a mud-purple grimace. A heart attack, but Maggie knew better.

He must have forgotten to ask for the phrase.

The adversaries had found him.

The Whistler set off through a building of twisting corridors and dusty dressing rooms, prop rooms and walkways. His heart clogged his throat. He had told James and Ursula to be careful, but had given them no chance to ask questions. He was aware with an acuteness like a blind knife that it would be such a hard discussion.

Better not to have it at all. Not before he knew if he was routed after all.

The corridors twisted insensibly until finally, one long hall led to a door where a strip of light peered through the threshold. When it opened, it was to the dull brass of late sun and air that smelled of copper and stone. Waiting beyond was a dry brush desert, full of jagged volcanic rocks and withered, cringing plants, expanding ever downward toward some ledge.

The Whistler was so seldom afraid, so seldom shaken. Yet he shut that door with quiet hesitance, as if the sound of the latch would echo through the empty desert and alert something to his presence. As he walked, his breath hissed loudly, and the time on his watch was always just a little too close. It wasn't as if he hadn't known it would be the challenge of his life to finally knit together the designs, these designs for which he had spent so many years laying the groundwork, yet he hadn't expected opposition from this angle. Not so soon. Not nearly so soon.

The lip of the desert curved down and became a sliding cone of sand and rock, angled toward an unseen lower point. All around rose the ridges, distant and brown. The Whistler picked his way down, his polished loafers scratching and sliding on the rough stones, and his mouth was dry as a bone.

The sun stopped falling as he made his way to the base, like the tip of an inverted pyramid. Shapes blurred into view: a strange golden doorway, that which lied beyond blurry and invisible. Before it stood a figure like a shadow scraped up from the earth, unformed and dim. It shivered like a desert mirage. Beside it crouched the figure of a nude old man, thin like tissue paper, his hands and feet marked with cuts and scrapes that pierced his fragile, ancient body. He scratched in the dirt as the Whistler approached, and then looked up sharply. He had no eyes, yet the Whistler felt a discomfort under his non-gaze that he did not express.

"You're back so soon," said the Whistler to the shadow. "I thought you'd be occupied a little longer with that goose chase."

The shadow fluttered in the dead air, but did not speak. Instead the old man looked to it, then translated, "She says she knew as soon as you sent her away. You always were a snake."

"I get things done, dear," said the Whistler. "You would rather languish on your isle, century upon century, hour upon hour in waning glory. Someone had to make the choice. And who is this?"

The old man's voice warbled weakly. "Who do you think I am?"

"An inconvenience. A fool."

The old man spat and shook his head. "You are the fool. I came to the isle because your ilk seek to end it all. I seek to save this world from those raven-thinkers who welcome the end, or you who hasten it."

The Whistler looked upon the man with pity and disdain. "You, like my dear Meliora, are a withered thing. Thin and weak, pretending at a fading glory. Someone had to make the choice."

The man sneered, his hatred a physical thing, bulbous and palpating. "She says, it was not your choice to make."

"Then whose was it?"

"If you unchain the stars, you and she will drift into the void, and there will be nothing left. Nothing you built, nothing you knew. Your people, your stories. Their lives rotten, then dust." The old man's legs trembled, as if his mere presence took a great toll on him.

"Yours or mine, why should I care?" said the Whistler with a smile. "My dear, we are dead. We have been dead for all time. Soon there will be no more choices to make, because we will be worn so thin there will be nothing left. Dead in all but name."

The old man spat again, viscous and thick. His hair was but tufts of dead grass on his head, his teeth snarled in years of anger and regret. "You've lost," he hissed. "You know you've lost, despite this grandstanding."

The shadow flickered, and in that moment took the image of someone standing in half-darkness: the body of a woman, graying and heavy-set, with turquoise bangles at her throat and wrists like an unrobbed Pharaoh. The ghastly image of poor Maggie Warner looked back at him like a corpse. The Whistler closed his fists in a sudden, unexpected rage, an anger to which he hadn't realized he could be inspired.

"After all I did for us, after all I did to save our people," he said, "you would do this? Insult me like this?"

The shadow only shuddered like leaves in a foreboding wind. The old man whispered, "She says she once believed your path to be the only way. But now she has learned that there is another route. She is more than willing to trap you and sever you from our world once and for all. She has your body, after all, unless you would return and best her."

Horror welled up, a foreign and choking emotion. *To live forever in dream, wrapped in those fine gold links of destiny.* "I highly doubt you can do that."

"I don't need you to believe me," said the old man with implacable rationality. "I am the sculptor. I will seal you in amber and sever dream from reality. Meliora has told me that this is what I was prophesied to do. You should know; you were there when that prophecy was spoken."

The stone, tilted away from the Tomb. Those catacombs, piled with statuary and gold. That body he had pointed to her, and entrusted her with that knowledge. Rage boiled up like a fountain of blood, and the Whistler walked to the old man, crouching like an insect in the dust, and placed his foot on the man's shoulder. With a kick, he shoved him backwards, so that the man's frail form sprawled in the dirt. The old man coughed and laughed, an ancient cackle, and the shadow just shivered. The Whistler breathed heavily as the old man pointed up at him, cackling.

"Stop your fool's errand," the old man said. "You know you can not best us, unless you would see yourself trapped and your host destroyed. Join us, or lay down your arms."

The Whistler took some steps back, sweat beading like cold venom at the back of his neck. He rubbed his chin, the bristling stubble scraping against his rough fingers. He could not go with them. It was beyond arrogance, beyond pride. It was not only his designs, which now fractured under the strain like glass, but that he had sworn he would not return to the place she was from until it was done. In truth, he didn't know what would be left of that which he'd left behind.

So when he spoke, it was with great heaviness.

"Very well," the Whistler said. "You win. I'll undo everything I've done. It will slide back into nothing. You can have each of them that I can return. The Arcaneum will be locked, the key returned, the language unspoke. I will undo all that led to the sacrifice that would wake what is in the Tomb, and resurrect it from half-dead. I will see to it that each is undone. But I will not go with you. I spent too long on that isle."

The old man looked again at the shadow. The dead form of the woman faded, and the shadow became mere darkness again. "She says this is a fair deal, Whistler," said the old man. "But she will be watching to ensure that it is all deconstructed."

The Whistler made a deferential bow, theatrical yet conceding. "I will undo all that it is in my power to undo. By the week's end, so long as there is no one who kills the bull, it will all be washed away as if by a flood."

The old man nodded. "Then I will close those doors now," he said. "Before any more mischief can occur."

"Now?"

"Yes. Now."

Like drifting upward in water, the dream began to lighten, those woven threads graying and fading.

Maggie found herself returning, and struggled to dive deeper, to return to the Whistler and be him, but there was no stopping her buoyant ascent. The light grew brighter and harsher, and the last image she recalled from the dream was of the Whistler meeting the eyes of that shadowed woman, the one who had stolen her form to mislead her affiliates. An understanding passed between them, and then Maggie was awake, insensate and inconsolable.

He was gone. He was truly gone. She could barely feel him anymore, and that sense of being at home, of being oneself had slipped away such that she could barely remember it. How had she been fooled, anyway? She clenched her fists with their small, doughy fingers, felt the heaviness of her chest and the smooth roundness of her face, and wondered how stupid she could have been to have thought there was another way. Some things were immutable. Some things couldn't be transfigured.

Lying in her bed, staring at the rough ceiling, she contemplated the old habits. Perhaps there was one that would end it entirely, and she would never again have to know the sick sensation of waking from a dream. As she rolled over to bury her face in the pillow, she felt something in bed next to her.

It was the crinkling of a slip of yellowed paper, and she pulled it free and studied it. Words crawled like worms across it, written in a hand that was not hers and yet was as familiar as if it were. Despite the language that she certainly couldn't read, she knew what it said. *"Make him pay,"* it read, and suddenly that crushing, wallowing despair took on a honed edge, heavy metal transformed into a lethal blade. He had left her a final message.

Maggie Warner knew that she was through. The busybodies were right—she couldn't keep doing this, not forever, not at all. But that didn't mean there wasn't one other thing to be done before she stopped. There was a cliff before her, dark water at the base and she had no idea how much of it was full of rocks. But before she took the plunge, there was someone she needed to wrap her arms around, lead blindly to the edge. When she fell, she would not be falling alone.

In the center of town was her stage. It was cut from rough white wood, and strung from it were bright plastic streamers and silk flowers, something exuberant turned gaudy through excess. The actors dressed in the makeshift backstage, gossiping in hushed tones while the tech crew made their final checks, tested the lights, rustled the curtains. Some cue was wrong; it was fine, they'd just work around it. One of the sets which had been done had been taken back in for touch-up, and wasn't finished. That was fine as well. They'd work around that, too. People were missing; where were their understudies? The signs of the shadow's sabotage were all around, a crippling insult.

As the parade wound through the town, approaching to the bouncy beat of Hailey Temple's most recent country hit, Maggie Warner knew that the acrobats would be flipping through the streets, and people would remember seeing their float with joy, and then shock. One of them would have fallen by now because of the changes to the route. The rhythm would be off. The music sounded off, tinny and robotic.

Above the stage rose 'Spirition, framing the whole performance like a finger pointed in defiance to the sky. The pictures that would be taken could have been postcards for years to come, remembered as one of the best things the town had seen. *Remember when we put on that massive celebration that year? Remember how much fun we had? What a town we are!* was the legacy that should have been.

But it wouldn't. It wasn't perfect. The celebration was falling apart in decay. Inside every set and streamer, it was all dead, and it would be remembered as such.

Through the week, Maggie had felt the Whistler undo his months of work like watching a plant slowly die and being unable to save it. Bit by bit, all the preparations fell flat and listless, sucked of their life and vigor. It was as if they had all been held up by strings, and now they were being loosened one by one. It would be a stillbirth. She knew it in her bones.

The crowd was subdued, as if they could sense the death behind the fluttering curtain. She hobbled through the backstage with a clipboard, checking over costumes, microphones, lighting cues, before the parade would lead the town into the central square of the amusement park and the show would begin in earnest.

"Maggie!" It was Linda Neuman again, that bit actor. Maggie turned away from the tech director reluctantly, twisting her face into a warm greeting. "There you are." She took a judgmental look at the crutch. "Are you sure you should be walking on that?"

Maggie rolled her eyes good-naturedly. "The doctor said it was fine to be up and about. And that's why I have the crutch, so I don't have to put weight on it. How's the parade coming, is it on its way?"

"It's just passing by the bank," said Linda, miffed. "They were having some trouble getting started, the float you commissioned last minute wouldn't attach to the truck bed quite right. They got it going, though."

There was a barb in there, but Maggie ignored it, just nodded. Another few minutes. "Have you seen Bill around?" she asked, and Linda got a look on her face like someone opening a fan to disguise interest. "He said he'd meet me back here before the show started."

"Oh, good!" said Linda. "You've made up, then, I'm glad to hear it. He mentioned that you seemed—"

Maggie laughed, waved it off. Linda would get her due. "Mad? Well, I don't really like being surprised, Linda. But yes, we reached an understanding after Wednesday. He said he'd be coming to wish me luck—"

And then there he was, picking his way through the stage crew all in tragedian black, his scalp pale in the too-bright sun.

"Mags, hey. Everything coming together?" he said, and Maggie smiled. He was, in his middle-aged way, still handsome, still with those kind creases around his eyes. He had an honest face without any guile. He had never needed such a thing, and it showed in him like a plain light left on.

"Just wanted to show you how I've been delegating," Maggie said to him. Linda gave her a raised-brow look and turned away to leave the pair alone. "No, really. I mean, could be better, but I gave it a try. And take a look at how it came together."

Miserable. Miserable. A dead and lifeless thing. A sick laughter welled within her. The actors lacked spark, and through the town the music grew louder, twisting and rotted. Bill was impressed, admiring. He never could keep up with her, nor wanted to, and for a time that had been fine. "It's incredible, Mags," he said, and put a hand on her shoulder in that way he did, the way men did to women they owned, and she shrugged it off, then patted his arm. She was compelled to play the part, to assuage that damage.

"Yeah, I'm pretty pleased," she said. "And I wanted to ask you. I have a line on stage at the end, as the show runner. Since it's a play about the town. I wanted you to come up with me."

Bill balked, tongue pressed in his cheek. "I don't know, won't that screw everything up? I mean I—"

"It's an acknowledgment," lied Maggie. "I mean, you read an early draft. It's a play about people working together in this town, so I have a line about being supported, and I want you to be there for it. I have a lot of people to thank, so I want you to be highlighted." Perhaps Maggie was the real actor, she considered with a bitter humor, as those cloying words rolled off her tongue. Maggie, yes, Maggie was the actor. This body was the character, and there was only make-believe behind it. That was how that character had been played by someone else, leading his affiliates astray.

"But won't I get in the way?"

"I'm running the thing, Bill, you won't get in the way at all. I think it'll be really nice."

She recalled the failing days of their relationship. Bill was such a man in so many ways, and there were all those little things he got away with that had stuck like burrs. It wasn't even that he was a sexist: he did his fair share, he was sensitive. It was deeper. What was it? Maggie had spent those days ruminating on them, on all those little expressions. The possessive hand on her knee. All the little instances in which he knew best, in which his knowledge was unshakable, in which he had it all figured out and it was up to her to acquiesce and assume that he was probably right and she had been infantile and foolish. Yes, we should take this street rather than another. The sound in the car was probably nothing. Yes, more sleep would probably fix the thing that was nagging at her.

It could be worse, it could always be worse. But it wasn't even that he was a man. It was that she—

The music grew louder, the twang, the excitement. The crowd murmured and hummed, and Maggie smoothed down her blouse and its incorrect folds, wishing for a cool breeze. Anything to break this unrelenting heat.

"Sure, I mean, if you want me to," said Bill. "If it means that much to you."

Maggie smiled at him. "Thanks, Bill."

"Mags?"

She looked up at him and resented his height.

"I'm proud of you for taking a break."

Then the music spilled into the square as the parade approached. Floats peeled off, but the acrobats and the music flipped through the crowd, waving patriotic ribbons and streamers. On the stage they did their final set to Hailey Temple's "Trapped in a Song," concluding with applause, polite and formal. Then it was time for the play to start.

The Winsome Daughter began with a song, one of Hailey Temple's early nostalgic tracks that Maggie had selected with such care. The first act was about the founding of the town, famous figures from its folklore, as Hailey's voice wound tinnily around the square. The crowd watched with some interest, though the expressions on faces changed as the lead struggled with their new lines, the delivery stilted. People wandered away from the square. The plot seemed to ramble, and if Maggie had been able to consider it, maybe it had never been that good a play, and had gotten worse through revision. Maggie had never had a flop before. It was fortunate, then, that none of this was real. It was a nightmare, and she could wake from a nightmare.

It wasn't that Maggie ever hated Bill. Frankly, she admired him for being the one person who could hold her to account. In a manner, it was a rare honor.

Olyoke

As the play progressed, the sense of being watched crept over Maggie, and she did her best not to show that she had noticed. The Whistler was miserably gone, but she wondered if perhaps (perhaps) that other being was checking in, ensuring that the Whistler had done as he said he would. Maggie feigned ignorance, merely spoke with Bill and watched as the play wandered through the years, through the roaring 20s and the logging days, to the construction of Hailey Land, into the modern day. Then finally, finally, the play reached its end. There was applause, generous and underwhelmed. It would be talked about after as a failure of expectation, the one time Maggie Warner had missed.

Once upon a time, that would have been enough to destroy her. Now she felt it like a clinging thread severed, a release leading to free fall. It hadn't been good enough, and she hadn't been good enough, and she had been right. It was time she exited stage left.

At last, Maggie's cue was given, and she took Bill's hand.

The glare from the spotlights and the brilliant sun was sweltering. Maggie waved as the crowd clapped, and Bill gave a nervous nod. On stage was the set of the Splitridge Swamp, bisected by an arching tree. It had once crawled with the ancient language James had painted beneath its skin, and now it was dead, unspoken. Maggie never became nervous before a crowd, but her breath caught in her throat at the severity of it all. She had been entrusted to see this through, by the person she would rather be.

"I just wanted to thank you all for being here today," Maggie Warner said, sun glinting off a sea of unmemorable faces. "This play has been a special project of mine for a long while now, and nothing has made me happier than seeing it come together as a part of this celebration. You all—" and she gestured to the crowd, and then she gestured to the actors and acrobats, the stage crew and techs, "—are unreal."

Applause went up, drowning out the music. When the claps and cheers faded, there was no more country twang, just some lower part of the track—all bells and clangs, rhythm without tune. Something moved on the outside of the sunlight, which made no sense because there was no shadow and no edge to it.

"And I want to give a special little nod to Bill Haxson, for supporting me through this." She looked at him, that plain, solid man, and he smiled with an embarrassed heat, and there was still a flutter of her heart. She had never hated him, after all, but she had simply not been able to stand his incomprehension. Perhaps that was all it was. He had looked at her and seen something that she wasn't, and that had driven them apart. "He's a man of incredible patience, gratitude, honesty, and compassion, and he exemplifies everything this town has to offer, and everything it is going to lose."

Broken applause, scattered but willing to give her the benefit. The line didn't land—what did that mean, had she misspoken?

"For that reason, I'd like to honor him here today with a quote from the play that inspired me to write this one," said Maggie Warner, and led Bill toward the center of the stage, toward the front. There, James waited anxiously just before the crowd, holding the package, and Maggie met his eyes and winked. "As you know if you've taken any of my classes, Jeremy Ries, our town's greatest playwright, is a favorite of mine."

Maggie positioned Bill in front of the painted tree and took both his hands behind his back. Only a moment of confusion passed before it was too late, and his wrists were bound tightly with the zip tie she had hidden in her pocket.

"Maggie, what's going on?" he said, but he wasn't wired for sound, and the crowd was not so close as to be able to see his reaction clearly.

Maggie held his arm tightly so that he could not turn, and if he felt her grip was stronger than it should have been, he didn't think to react as he should. Maggie projected out to the crowd in thespian dramaticism, a sweeping gesture and step toward that bundle which James now held in his hands, concealed in cloth.

" 'Dark things do not frighten me as much as the running fire— Oh, no tears!' " she incanted. The sound of metal clanging and bells tolling echoed over the square like a misplaced word. Maggie traced a finger beneath Bill's eye, as if he had shed a tear. " 'Do you mourn the red leaves of autumn? Do you decry the spring? I do not believe this is a dark thing, my love.' "

Something shuddered in the crowd, something that caused people to look down by their feet. Maggie started, knowing she had little time, as titters and confusion rose up. With a dramatic fall to a knee, she said the final line, " 'Rather, I see it as joyous. An occasion.' " And she took the wrapped weapon from James, who looked at her with an emotion so strange—a fear, and an anticipation, and an elation. Maggie suddenly wanted to show the boy that it would be alright, that it would come together.

But she didn't hear the roar of the crowd as it appeared, if there was one at all, because the sound of metal and bells was louder, and the rush of some great wind from the heights came howling down. The celebration was here, and a new procession was coming like a planarian worming through the streets.

"How did you do it?" demanded the old man. He rose from the ground like a horrid blossom, emerging, his face alive with anger. James recoiled from him with disgust and curiosity, as around them the crowd disappeared into the background like an unneeded set-piece, whisked away by an unseen crew. "I told you to take it all apart. I watched you do it."

"All my loves are sweet idiots," Maggie said, meeting the man's eyes and running her hand along Bill's shoulders. As she did, she seemed to slide into her skin until it belonged, not merely some costume she was wearing. It came with the humor of the Whistler, and the rough maleness that fit her without pain. "That seems to be my type."

"Tell me," the old man demanded. "Tell me now how you allowed it past the stars."

"Here's a secret for you," said Maggie, and addressed Bill, who looked at her with confusion. The unreality crept behind his eyes—he had never been real, had he, just a placeholder, and wasn't it a shame? He smelled of sandalwood, summer sweat, and kindling, and seemed so young, now. "All the flags and dancers, the *performance* . . . all this is decoration. Don't get me wrong, I love a birthday party as much as the next man. But for a celebration in this town, there's only one thing you really have to do."

The skin around Bill's eyes was yellow, sagging and dripping in the impossibly bright light. On the ground, the old man sweated, his mouth an angry O.

Maggie Warner smiled like a light turning on. "All you have to do is kill the bull."

The procession spilled into the square in advance of what approached. Bells rang and whistles called, and that light so impossibly bright burned hotter and hotter. If the unreal crowd still watched as Maggie pushed Bill to his knees and then his chest, if the bystanders clutched each other in confusion, Maggie didn't know and didn't care. The ax fell swiftly in the glinting sun, and the blow was sudden.

Was there a gasp from the crowd at the convincing prop work? Was there a scream as they realized that none of this was an act? Did the procession arrive in glory and celebration, heralding the return of two things long parted from each other, and did the shadow of the unreal world quiver and tremble before it?

The head, lifted above the stage in triumph, looked at Maggie Warner with sweet surprise. The Whistler lifted it to his lips and drank, and it tasted of copper and honey. A kiss between men was such a different way of loving.

ACKNOWLEDGEMENTS

I have to thank Zabé, first and foremost. You single-handedly pushed me to be a better writer and actually finish drafts. Thank you John, for being the one to tell me first about spotted lanternflies and their strange red nymphs, and for reading many drafts of this book. Your taste is impeccable and your advice always sage. Sol, you are my beloved friend who keeps me abreast of industry things I do not have the time for but really need to know. I can't wait for you to finish your manuscript and blow us all out of the water. Robin, our relationship is not predicated on liking each other's art, though it's quite a bonus that we do.

Thank you to everyone who's been there with me from the start: Deb & Dave, Emme, Ashley, Grace, Aunt Donna, and many more. Many apologies if I have forgotten a beta reader somewhere. Rick, I think you should be in here, too.

The team at Tenebrous, Alex and Matt, is incredible. I'm very glad you took a chance on a debut author. It's a great fortune to find a press that completely understands one's Weird, Weird work and brings it to life. I'm still very delighted that Alex and I share a love of *Pathologic*.

Lastly, I have to credit Katherine for showing me the Codex Seraphinianus and telling me about your journey to Pigeon Forge, which clearly made an indelible impact.

ABOUT THE CONTRIBUTORS

Vincent Endwell is a writer, composer, and researcher originally hailing from unceded Onondaga territory (Central New York). Their work has been previously published in Campfire Publishing, Radon Journal, and Dark Horses Magazine, among others. Over the years, they have grown less certain that they would like to see a ghost.

Jenna Cha is an artist and writer. In 2017 she graduated from the Minneapolis College of Art and Design and [redacted] a degree in Comic Art. In 2019 she made her debut publication as the co-creator/artist for the Stoker-longlisted series *BLACK STARS ABOVE*, written by Lonnie Nadler and published by Vault Comics. Her current ongoing horror series, *THE SICKNESS*, is co-written by Lonnie Nadler and published by Uncivilized Books.

Echo Echo is a Portuguese artist and a proponent of *horror vacui*. She immerses herself in individual pieces for up to a year at a time and renders in extreme detail. Echo also performs in multiple bands, finding equal freedom in expressing herself through music as she does through illustration.

Publisher's Note:

"Love in the Reem" first appeared in *Eat Your Heart Out, Vol. One*, originally published by Campfire Press in February 2025.

WEIRD TIMES DEMAND WEIRD READS:

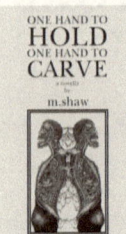

ONE HAND TO HOLD, ONE HAND TO CARVE
M.Shaw

Two halves of a human cadaver awaken on a cold morgue slab, remembering nothing of their previous existence as a singular body. Their impending schism will lead them on separate and frightening paths forward.

A Weird, surreal Body Horror journey; Wonderland Award Winner for Best Novel, 2023.
"Bold, grotesque and oddly touching" - Andy Davidson

FROM THE BELLY
Emmett Nahil

A strange man is found alive within the belly of a whale. He is rescued and brought aboard the whaling ship, where a series of accidents, deaths and horrific transformations immediately begin sweeping through the crew. Now they must contend with the vengeance of the sea made flesh, as well as the consequences of their own greed and destruction.
"A taut work of horror" - Publisher's Weekly

CASUAL
Koji A. Dae

In a dystopian near-future, Valya manages her anxiety with the help of her neural implant, CASUAL. But now she is pregnant, and the law forbids her from using CASUAL as sole caregiver to her unborn child. Her returned panic attacks have her considering a controversial clinical trial that would place a tandem device in her vulnerable child. *Casual* is a stark and cutting glance at a near future that looks uncannily like our present.
"Up there with Atwood, Bradbury, Dick, and Gibson"
- Literary Hub

PUPPET'S BANQUET
Valkyrie Loughcrewe

Married couple Celia and Martin are brutally attacked on their drive through the Irish countryside. The attack leaves Celia with a violent schism in her mind, seemingly existing in two places at once: one the "real" world, the other a howling, monstrous maelstrom. Of her husband, there is no trace...until weeks later, when he is discovered in a bizarre hospital, his body spliced together with that of an unknown woman...and they are very pregnant.
"Not for the faint of heart, but its impact is undeniable."
- Booklist

REEF MIND
Hazel Zorn

The coral reef rose from the seas, spreading across the land with incredible speed.
A rapidly evolving invasive species.
It transformed the landscape.
Mutated every living creature of the surface world.
We never suspected it had a plan.

"A new voice in Weird Horror worth keeping a close eye on."
- Michael Wehunt

TURN TO TENEBROUS.

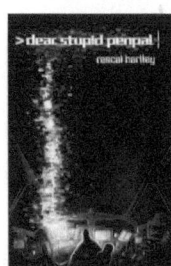

DEAR STUPID PENPAL
Rascal Hartley

Atticus hates space, hates the ship, hates his fellow astronauts. He makes that painfully clear in his letters to Aku, his corporate-assigned penpal back on Earth.
But as the mission continues into deeper space, time begins moving all wrong. As everyone else's penpals rapidly die of old age, Finch turns, heartbroken, to Aku; who, more than a century later, is somehow still there.

"Joyously weird and unexpected" - Íde Hennessey

KAYAK
Kristal Stittle

Keith's kayak is his only means of survival. Solid ground means certain death at the scissor-claws of vicious invading creatures. What he needs is to find more people; but terrible guilt anchors him in solitude. A year earlier, when the creatures first appeared, Keith's choices brought disaster to the island community that took him in. Now it's time to take responsibility...if he survives.

"Grips you by the throat and doesn't let go"
- Max Booth III

SOFT TARGETS
Carson Winter

Two office drones discover a loophole that makes some days less real—less permanent—than others, and start to act out their violent fantasies without fear of reprisal. Why shouldn't they? Tomorrow, everything will go back to normal, with no one the wiser but them.
Now their jokes about taking a bullet to get off work early—or pulling the trigger themselves—just became a whole lot more real.

"A hell of a story...and damned funny" - Jon Padgett

WE LIKE IT CHERRY
Jacy Morris

Documentarist Ezra Montbanc hits the jackpot when he receives an invitation to document the rites of a mysterious, unknown Indigenous tribe who reside in the harrowing, inhospitable Arctic.
It's a shot at the prestigious journalism career he's long envisioned, and a path out of the exploitative career he's grown embittered with.
But Ezra and his crew soon find themselves in a frozen and bloody battle for survival atop an inaccessible glacier ritual site, where men and mythical horrors hunger for sacrifice.

"Not for the faint of heart. Morris' narrative does not pull punches"
- Booklist, starred review

FIND YOUR NEXT TENEBROUS TITLE. STAY WEIRD.
TENEBROUSPRESS.COM

CONTENT WARNINGS

Being a work of mature Horror, a degree of violence, gore, sex and/or death is to be expected.

At the author's request, the following warnings are also offered:

"Modeling Resin"—children imperilment & death
"Wandering Daughter"—mention of children imperilment, death, fire
"Scratch"—contagion, pet death
"Itch"—contagion, self-harm, compulsion
"Love in the Reem"—contagion
"Isle of the Dead"—derealization
"Pyramid"—death of a family member
"The Celebration"—violent death, derealization

Please be advised.

More information at
www.tenebrouspress.com

Home of New Weird Horror, New Weird Dark Fiction, Oddities, Abnormalities and All Manner of Eccentricities You Never Knew You Needed More Than Oxygen

FIND OUT MORE:

www.tenebrouspress.com

@TenebrousPress on social media

HAIL THE TENEBROUS CULT

www.ingramcontent.com/pod-product-compliance
Lightning Source LLC
LaVergne TN
LVHW040055080526
838202LV00045B/3653